Something broke loose inside her, something she'd held back for almost a year.

"You protect. I heal, Booker." She touched a finger to the lock of hair on his forehead, then brushed it back, testing his limits. "Let me try to do my job."

When he didn't move, she leaned in, then up until their lips almost touched. "Maybe I'll heal us both in the process," she whispered.

With a groan, he pulled her to him. His mouth covered hers, just as she wanted, just as she remembered.

Desire tumbled free, caught between them, pushed and pulled by longing, need…months of loneliness.

He took, she gave, until the air thickened, the edges of reality blurred.

She'd missed him, missed this. His arms tightened, drawing her into his lap as if he'd missed her, too.

Suddenly Booker broke
her back, pointed at the

D1400744

DONNA YOUNG

BODYGUARD LOCKDOWN

◆ **HARLEQUIN**® INTRIGUE®

To Kay Kelly
For your strength, love, wisdom and wicked sense of humor.
And for sharing with me your wonderful memories of my
parents, my grandparents and our families.
You know Uncle John is smiling….
Happy birthday, Aunt Kay. I love you.

ISBN-13: 978-0-373-74745-0

BODYGUARD LOCKDOWN

Recycling programs
for this product may
not exist in your area.

Copyright © 2013 by Donna Young

HARLEQUIN®
™ www.Harlequin.com

Printed in U.S.A.

ABOUT THE AUTHOR

Donna Young, an incurable romantic, lives with her family in beautiful Northern California.

Books by Donna Young

HARLEQUIN INTRIGUE
824—BODYGUARD RESCUE
908—ENGAGING BODYGUARD
967—THE BODYGUARD CONTRACT
1016—BODYGUARD CONFESSIONS
1087—SECRET AGENT, SECRET FATHER
1106—A BODYGUARD FOR CHRISTMAS
1148—CAPTIVE OF THE DESERT KING
1310—BLACK OPS BODYGUARD
1424—BODYGUARD LOCKDOWN

CAST OF CHARACTERS

Dr. Sandra Haddad—A world-renowned scientist. Driven by a past family tragedy, she's developed a rapid healing serum that will revolutionize modern medicine. Or kill millions of people…

Booker McKnight—A former black ops agent intent on revenge against the arms dealer who killed his family. It's taken him five years to set the trap. His bait? A beautiful research scientist. But when it comes time to spring the trap, can he risk the woman he loves, to destroy the man he hates?

General Riorden Trygg—An arms dealer, who will not stop short of world domination. The only obstacles in his way? A woman scientist, a former government agent and a small country or two.

Colonel Jim Rayo—He's ex-military with an aptitude for weapons and war. As a young soldier he swore allegiance to his commander. Now, decades later, when that commander turns out to be a fanatical arms dealer, does Rayo stand his ground…or get buried under it?

Chapter One

United States Disciplinary Barracks, Leavenworth

"Front and center, General." The order caught on Sergeant Tom Levi's tongue. A night of sour beer and stale peanuts left his mouth thick and woolly. It was 0500 hours, he was hungover and not in the mood for anyone's attitude.

"Now!" He banged the cell bars with his flashlight. Tiny sledgehammers pounded inside his skull, setting his teeth on edge.

Tom wasn't a lightweight. At five eleven, one hundred ninety pounds, he'd been able to hold his liquor since he was eighteen. Twenty years later, he could damn well do it without a splitting headache the next day.

The problem was he hadn't stopped at two beers. Somewhere during the second drink he'd lost track of time, ended up slamming more beers then blacked out.

He woke up in his car at four in the morning, half intoxicated, with his cell phone ringing.

His commander ordered him to report to the prison. Stat.

"Damn it, Trygg, get your butt up!" Tom snapped. Nausea churned in his gut and sharpened the dry grit that gouged at his eyes.

Feet shuffled slow and steady from the other side of the door, echoed by a slight cough that came with smoking expensive cigars. "What can I do for you this morning, Sergeant?"

"You have two minutes to get yourself presentable. I'm taking you to the commander."

It was a lie, of course. Transfer papers had hit the commander's desk last evening, ordering the prisoner, General Riorden Trygg, from Leavenworth, Kansas, to an undisclosed destination in Washington, D.C.

Before his arrest, the general had been dealing in military weapons on the side, supplying enemies with the means to kill American soldiers.

Any one of the soldiers in the prison would give a year in solitary confinement for thirty seconds with the man on the other side of the cell bars.

Hell, if it wasn't for his career, Tom would throw the bastard into a cell full of these guys. All of them had served overseas in their careers. And most had lost friends or family in combat.

Tom glanced at his watch. Two minutes were up. "Hal! Let's do this!"

Tom waited until Sergeant Harold Coffey joined him, shackles in hand. Slightly overweight with a bulldog face, Hal was known as the least intelligent of the group. But he had meat on him, enough to handle any prisoner who got out of line.

"Stand clear, Trygg. Hands on your head, knees on the floor," Tom ordered, then flashed his light into the cell.

After Trygg was in position, he opened the door.

Hal quickly secured the shackles and hoisted Trygg to his feet.

"What's really going on, Sergeant Levi?" Trygg questioned. "In the five years I've been here, the commander has never reported for duty before nine in the morning. Later, if he managed a night with his mistress."

"Shut up, Trygg. Or I'll shut you up." But the damage was done. Other inmates had heard the exchange.

"You finally taking the trash out, Levi?" yelled one of the prisoners. "Don't we get to watch him die in a few months?"

Tom ignored them and pushed Trygg forward.

The cell block erupted. Prisoners banged on their bars, spewing profanity and threats at the general.

Trygg shuffled forward, his back ramrod straight, his close-cropped hair snow-white and meticulously neat.

The general's features remained emotionless.

His square jaw balanced the low brow, the deep-set azure eyes.

Not surprising. Riorden Trygg, while a traitor to his country, was still a military man through and through.

They passed through lockdown security, and followed the procedure of being scanned.

A few minutes later, the three men stepped out onto the compound parking area. A predawn mist, heavy from days of rain, blanketed the concrete yard, settled through the high barbed-wire fences.

Tom directed Trygg toward the armored truck—army issued, muddy green and no windows—parked just beyond the exit.

Two guards stood at the back bumper. Their rifles ready, their eyes scanning the perimeter.

Tom turned to the nearest guard. "Ready?"

"Yes, sir."

"Let's go," he ordered Trygg, and then nudged the older man forward.

The vehicle door stood open, revealing a long, narrow path inside, flanked by two benches and a thin window separating the driver and cab at the far end.

Tom shackled the general's hardware to a bolted iron bar on the floor, pushed him onto one bench and then sat across from him on the other.

Harold settled next to the general.

"So where are we going, Sergeant Levi?"

"Where the army wants you."

"Fair enough." Trygg smirked, his cool blue eyes sweeping over Tom. "You look like you had a rough night."

Tom said nothing. He had no windows to look out, except for a small slit facing the driver's cab. Regulation wouldn't have permitted him to anyway. He needed both eyes on his prisoner.

Fifteen minutes later, the truck stopped. Plane engines roared outside, vibrating the concrete beneath the vehicle's tires.

"Sounds like I'm going quite a distance," Trygg commented, then purposefully glanced at Tom's watch. "Or maybe not anywhere at all."

Without warning, gunfire burst from outside on the tarmac. Bullets ripped through the front windshield. The driver's head exploded, blood and gray matter spattered the slit window.

"Damn it!" Tom reached for his side arm. "That's bulletproof glass."

"New kind of ammunition," Trygg explained, his tone deceptively pleasant. "My men have had access to it for a couple months now."

"Your men—"

"Tom."

Tom's head snapped around. Harold leveled his pistol at Tom's chest. "You stupid son of a bitch!"

Red blotches mottled Hal's face. From anger or embarrassment, Tom couldn't be sure. But the man's hand remained steady, his jaw tight. "Money talks," Hal sneered.

"This isn't personal, Sergeant," Trygg commented, the blue of his eyes arctic, the pupils dilated and dark with malevolence. "You are in the wrong place at the wrong time."

A chilling calm rippled through Tom. So be it.

"You'll never live to see any payoff, Hal," Tom said, while his hand slipped slowly to his hip. "That's why Trygg offered the job to you. You're too stupid to realize it."

"But you weren't, Sergeant Levi. Which is why we drugged you a bit last night. Couldn't have you thinking with a clear head this morning, now could we?" Trygg acknowledged.

"How did you know I'd be assigned?"

When the general smirked, Tom swore. Inside job. High up.

Suddenly angry, Tom grabbed for his pistol. But his fingers barely touched the metal grip when Harold fired.

"Who's stupid now?" Hal watched his friend fall to the floor, then retrieved the shackle keys from his belt.

Hal unlocked the chains and Trygg rubbed his wrists. It was a shame really, Trygg thought, studying Tom's body on the floor. He could have used someone like Sergeant Levi in his unit. Smart. Talented. Just too much patriotic idealism for Trygg's plans.

"Ready, General?"

Nothing like the poor excuse for a soldier standing in front of him.

"Not quite yet, Sergeant." Trygg grabbed Tom's pistol, pointed and pulled the trigger three times.

Hal slumped back against the wall, a trail of blood gushing from his throat as he struggled for breath. Trygg shrugged. "Unfortunately for you, Sergeant Levi was right."

A fist pounded the truck's side. "All clear, General?"

"Yes, Colonel. Situation is controlled." Trygg dropped the pistol, stepped over the two dead bodies and stood toward the front of the truck.

"Clear!"

The two doors exploded, knocking Trygg slightly off his feet. His hand shot out, found the wall, and he steadied himself.

Then the acid edge of gunpowder sliced through the air, burned his nostrils. He stepped toward the door. The frigid morning air slapped at him.

"Smell that, Jim?" He took a deep breath, looked at the man waiting at the step of the truck. "Know what that is?"

"No, sir," Colonel Jim Rayo answered honestly. He was a man of average height, with a barrel chest and a thick trunk that left little room for more than a squat neck under hard, weather-lined features and keen brown eyes.

Trygg jumped to the ground and slapped his friend on the shoulder. "That is the scent of freedom."

"We're not safe yet, General." Rayo's mouth thinned into a grim line, then nodded to a tan sedan a few yards away. "I have a plane waiting for us at a private airstrip nearby. We should be in Taer by tonight."

"And the good doctor? Has she been detained?"

"Yes, sir." Rayo signaled the other men into their cars and led the general to his ride. "The men seized Doctor Sandra Haddad an hour ago."

"And?" Trygg asked, pausing at the car.

"You were right." Jim opened the passenger door. "She put up one hell of a fight."

"That's promising," Trygg replied. "After five years of waiting, I'd hate to think she'd make this easy for me."

Chapter Two

The storm hit the midnight air, a blistering squall of dust and grit that clogged lungs, cut into eyes and covered the empty city streets of Taer in desert sand.

Booker stepped into a nearby alley, ignoring the bite of the wind, the slap of grit against his face. Rage and impatience—and just enough uneasiness—kept his footsteps silent, his senses alert, his knife in his fist.

He was a tall man, long in the leg, lean in the hips, but broad in the shoulder and chest. He was hard muscled—and hardheaded, if a person listened to those who knew him.

He'd been born among the oil fields of Texas, spent his youth traipsing around the Chihuahuan Desert with his father, working when they could, fending off hunger when there were no jobs to be found. His mother died long before he could form vivid memories of her. But the vague ones, recollections of soft scents and softer words, he carried in the deepest part of his soul.

At eighteen, when the snap of a steel cable took his father's life, Booker traded the oil rigs for military combat zones, the searing heat of the desert for the muck and brush of the jungles and the beleaguered inner cities of third-world countries.

For twenty years, he breathed in the scent of blood, tasted its metallic bite against the back of his throat, choked on the acid remnants of gunpowder. Lived with the cries of the wounded and tortured in his nightmares.

A car roared past, skidded to a halt just down the street only yards back from his SUV.

Booker eyed the platinum finish, the sleek lines—the license plate.

Home-grown.

He shifted back into the shadows, confident his black shirt and trousers blended well with the darkness.

A young couple slid out of the car, darted up the deserted street, their heads down, their arms linked, laughing as they fought the wind.

Booker wondered if he'd ever been that young, or that carefree.

A door caught the wind, slammed against the wall. A string of curses hit the air. American.

Booker tightened his grip on the hilt of his knife.

A man walked past, his shoulders thick, his gait cautious. A black scarf covered his head, hung loose from the man's face. An AK-47 assault rifle rested in the crook of his arm.

Booker stepped behind the man, hooked his forearm around the exposed neck and yanked. The spine snapped, the muscles slackened. Booker dragged the body to the farthest part of the alley.

"Where are your friends?" Booker whispered, then tugged the scarf from the man's head, looped it around his own, leaving only his eyes uncovered.

He grabbed the machine gun and eased against the back door of the five-story apartment building. Three windows of the third-floor rooms flickered with lights and shadows.

Which room are you in, Doc?

An image of Doctor Sandra Haddad flashed through his mind.

Long, silky hair the color of a starless midnight sky, delicate features.

But it was her eyes—big and brown, intelligent-sharp— and the warm, sun-kissed skin that caught a man's eyes, stayed in his memory.

Haunted his dreams.

Booker tugged on the back door, found it locked.

The storm strengthened. A gust of wind slammed a nearby shutter against a second-story window. *One...two...*

He aimed the weapon at the lock. *Three.* Booker pulled the trigger. The lock burst.

He shifted his shoulder against the door and shoved.

No lights.

Booker waited in silence with machine gun raised, his eyes focused on the darkness just beyond.

A moment later shadows shifted, objects formed into patterns. He noted a hallway, the door at its end—the slit of light at its base.

Booker eased up to the door, heard nothing from the other side. The sharp scent of antiseptic cleaner and stale cigars slapped at him. Slowly, he swung the door open.

The lobby's light cast a dull yellow glow on a scuffed tile floor, bare gray walls. Rows of mail slots flanked the front entrance that fed across a long, narrow room and ended with a staircase against the far wall.

Booker made his way up the stairs to the third floor, his stance loose, poised.

Three men guarded the hallway. All ex-military, with the cropped hair, pumped-up muscles and sweat-stained military fatigues.

Two leaned outside one door, flanking its sides, while the other sat on the floor, head resting against the wall, his eyes closed—his finger on the trigger of the AK-47 in his lap.

An inner door slammed shut somewhere in the protected room. The first guard, a short man sporting a scar across one eye, smacked his buddy on the back and laughed. "I think Milo will have a good time. Then it will be our turn, no?"

"I would only kill her," the other growled, and limped toward the sleeping guard.

Her.

Sandra.

Rage rippled the air around him. Rage at her. More rage at himself for letting them take her.

The attack had been unexpected. He'd been too far from her. Had underestimated their speed, their abilities at the airport.

He wouldn't again.

The shortest of the three set his rifle against the wall. He wiped the sweat from his forehead with his sleeve, his meaty hands grimy and blood-spattered.

Sandra's delicate features, flawless skin—both, Booker imagined, now bloody and bruised.

Gritting his teeth, he buried the rage, the fear, the guilt, all where his other ghosts lurked. Down in the darkest corner of his soul.

"Hey," he whispered. The men swung around, surprised. He stepped into the hall, palmed his knife and threw it, all in one practiced motion.

With a sharp *thwap,* the blade imbedded in the limping man's throat. The man grasped at the handle while he choked on his own blood.

The sleeping man started awake. Booker kneed him in the face, transforming the man's warning cry into a pained grunt. With a twist on his head, he snapped the man's neck and turned.

"Come on." The shorter man kicked his machine

gun aside, his features twisted in derision. He motioned Booker closer with a wave of his fingers. "Let's play."

Booker snagged his knife from the dead man and lunged.

At the last second, he dropped, then rolled. Booker's foot rammed the other man's crotch. "Tag, you're it."

The man's knees buckled and he screamed.

"No?" Booker slammed him into the opposite wall. "Twenty questions, then. Is that the doc's blood on your hands?"

The mercenary struggled, his feet lost traction. Booker's hand tightened at his throat, cutting off his oxygen.

"I'll take that as a yes," Booker taunted against his enemy's ear. The scent of fear, of blood, of death permeated the air between them. Heavy. Sour.

"Game over." He shoved the knife up into the man's ribs and twisted. "You lose."

DOCTOR SANDRA HADDAD clawed through the shifting blackness, caught up in a whirlpool of nothingness and pain until the pain bit back, dragging its teeth across muscle and bone.

Sandra set her jaw, waited until the worst passed. Then she opened her eyes.

The darkness remained. Pitch-black and smothering. She felt it then, the heavy canvas against her nose and cheeks.

A hood.

She inhaled deeply through her nose until the scent of mildew and sour sweat choked off her breath.

Hysteria stirred at the back of her throat, making it difficult to breathe.

Her hands hung high above her head. Her arms twisted, locked in place by her weight. Trapped.

She bit her lip, kept the fear, the whimper of fear, deep in her chest. If her enemies were near, she didn't want to alert them.

Instead she concentrated on the silence beyond the cover, until her heartbeat slowed and the blood no longer pounded in her eardrums.

No sound meant no immediate danger. They weren't interested in her right now.

They.

Who were they?

The kidnapping happened so fast that it caught her off guard. The sound of the door slamming shut, the scrape of metal, the vile scent of unwashed bodies.

Three men? No four, she corrected. Including the driver. Their van tinted dark, their faces covered with ski masks. She remembered the squeal of tires, the short burst of bullets that strafed the asphalt, probably to terrorize anyone who thought of helping. They snatched her from the airport tarmac, less than twenty feet from boarding the plane.

She bolted under the plane's belly, but didn't get more than a few yards. When they grabbed her, she broke someone's nose with her elbow. Caught another in the instep of his foot, heard him cry out in pain when those bones gave.

Sandra clawed and jabbed and screamed and punched. But there were too many in the end. Blurred, shadowy features.

They injected her with a drug. She felt the pinch of the needle then remembered nothing else.

"So you are awake?"

The cover was jerked off her head. She blinked, her eyes adjusting to the sting of the bright light.

A man stood in front of her, a machine gun strapped to his back, the barrel tip jutting past his shoulder.

Dressed in a mixture of army fatigues and desert gear, the buttons of his shirt strained over a sagging belly, the tails loose and ripped at his waist. Both pants and shirt were stiff with dirt and sweat, and reeked of body odor.

"Good evening, Doctor Haddad." The man's gaze flipped up to her hands then down again. "Are you comfortable?"

Handcuffs, looped through a chain and anchored in the ceiling, cut into her wrists. Plastic ties dug into her ankles. Each secured to the sides of a steel folding chair. Small drops of blood slid over her ankle, tickled her skin.

"Extremely," Sandra mocked, but fear kept her chest tight, her voice high.

Perspiration coated his bald, flat features. His jawline sagged into a nasty grin, thinning out his big lips over gapped yellowed teeth.

But the dried blood that caked his swollen, broken nose told her they'd met before. On the tarmac.

"General Trygg will be here within a few hours," the man commented. "You can tell him how well you've been treated."

Sandra hadn't planned on staying that long. Trygg, while brilliant, was psychotic. And that wasn't a good combination.

"Does he treat all his guests this way?" She tried to lift her shoulders, give her wrists some reprieve.

The man shrugged. "I do not know. You are the first I've held for him. The others I have killed."

"That's reassuring." Sandra looked past the man's shoulder to the room beyond. Searching.

"Looking for this?" He held up a medical bag, its black leather worn and scratched. "Nothing in here will help you."

That much was true. She straightened her spine, lifted her chin. "I'm a doctor. My bag is essential—"

"You are a paycheck to me." With a flick, he tossed the bag onto a stained gold couch across the room. "Or an opportunity. Which will it be?"

"I have no idea what you are talking about."

"You put General Trygg on death row. But he wants you alive. And he is offering a substantial amount of money to keep you that way." He grabbed her chin, pinched the bones until she gasped. "Why go to Tourlay?"

"It's a border town. The last place he'd search," she scoffed. "Take it from me, anyone who helps Trygg ends up dead."

"Or rich." He laughed, then winced. His hand went to his nose, checked for blood.

"You should have that checked," Sandra quipped. "I know a good veterinarian."

He grabbed the collar of her blouse, drew her close until only his foul breath separated them. "You think you are safe until Trygg gets here? You are not."

Sandra slammed her forehead into his nose. The man staggered back bellowing. Blood smeared his face, dripped from his chin.

"Untie my hands," she spat. "We'll see who is safe from who."

"You bitch!" His fist came down. She tried to dodge the blow, but had nowhere to go. Pain exploded against the side of her temple, ricocheted through her shoulder as her chair toppled over.

She bit her lip against her scream, refusing to give him the satisfaction.

The handcuffs held her, kept her knees from

touching the ground. Her ankles remained bound to the chair's deadweight.

He grabbed her hair, yanked her head back. A knife appeared in his hand, the cold steel pressed against the delicate curve of her throat. "I could kill you now and be gone before Trygg walks through the door."

"You'll be hunted down like the rodent you are," Sandra managed, her voice rough, her jaw set against the pain. "You have no idea who you are dealing with."

"Neither do you, Dr. Haddad," he snarled.

Without warning, the man jerked. Air burst from his mouth; surprise widened his eyes, slackened his jaw.

He slid to the floor without another sound, a knife protruding from the back of his skull.

"Honey, I'm home." The soft Texan drawl reached her.

Sandra's eyes snapped up, took in the black scarf that hid all but the ice-blue eyes.

"Booker?" Recognition, then relief came swiftly, followed by the pinch of tears and a shudder in her chest.

The sharp jab of uncertainty took a full second more. "How did you find me?"

"I followed the trail of stupidity." He retrieved his knife from the dead body, wiped the blood on the man's shirt, then straightened. "Why aren't you safe at the palace?"

"You think this was my fault?"

"It isn't?" He tugged the scarf from his face, left it on the floor beside her.

"Only *you* would blame me for getting kidnapped."

Sandra took in the harsh, unbending features, the sculpted lips that rarely curved into a smile.

There'd been a time when love made his words kind, humor softened the sharp planes of his face. This was not it.

"You are one of the royal physicians. You live at the palace, surrounded by security. By family. And instead, when threatened, you go to the airport late at night, alone. Making yourself an easy target."

Pride kept her from responding. Along with the small sliver of truth in his words.

Still, she had her reasons.

He sliced through the binds at her feet with the knife, sheathed the blade, then placed his hands at her waist. "Stand up. I'll keep you steady. Don't lock your knees or you'll faint."

"I'm the one with the medical degree. Not you," she snapped, more impatient with herself than him. The longer it took her to recover, the longer they were in danger.

The position took the weight off her wrists. Blood rushed in, setting both on fire. When her knees buckled, he swore. Then brought her against him, held her steady.

"Give it a minute," he ordered, the words harsh, the warmth of his body solid, reassuring.

It had always been that way. The strength of his arms, the force of his will. The only time in her life she'd truly felt safe.

The only time she'd truly felt anything.

"Try it again." His hands gently gripped her hips, eased her away.

Her legs trembled, but held her weight. After giving them a moment, Sandra straightened. The pressure eased from her wrists, left her arms weak.

"Hold still. I'm almost done." Booker pulled a handcuff shim from his watchband. His hands stretched to meet hers, his touch gentle but urgent.

Hip to hip, chest to chest, the air thinned, then hummed. But this time Sandra ignored the quakes that rippled down her back, kept her legs rubbery.

"Got it," he murmured.

Her arms dropped and she cried out. A thousand needles stabbed at her. Sandra bit her lip, unable to lift either limb.

He sat her in the chair, then took her right wrist between his palms and rubbed. "You've been tied up for a long time. This is going to hurt."

Sandra gasped as the needles morphed into white-hot knives, slicing through every nerve to the muscles beneath.

"Fight through it." Booker didn't let up. Rubbing her skin, forcing her blood to move beneath.

Seconds turned into a minute, then two. Her jaw tightened against another torrent of stabs and spasms. "This is taking too much time."

"Let me worry about that." He dropped one arm and grabbed the other. His hands worked the blood flow, warming her skin, soothing the needles beneath.

"You can stop now," she whispered, her voice hoarse from the pain or something far more dangerous. She couldn't be sure. Didn't want to find out.

She tugged her arm free. "I'm much better. Let's go."

Her chin shot up; her eyes dared him to argue.

Booker didn't. Instead, he took in her ivory silk blouse, the matching dress slacks. Both cool in the heat, and a dead giveaway in the dark.

He glanced at her shoes, noted the flat, thinly strapped sandal over the feminine arch, the delicate ankle. "No wonder they caught you."

"I wasn't thinking 'desert escape' when I dressed this morning."

"And yet, getting on a plane unprotected was your logical solution," Booker countered. "You have an IQ bigger than my phone number, Doc. You couldn't come up with a better strategy?"

"I had little time and very few choices," she snapped.

"You could have asked me for help."

Lord knew she'd thought about it. Almost called him twice. In a laboratory or with a patient, he'd never question her skill. In danger, she should have never questioned his ability to protect her.

No one knew Riorden Trygg better than Booker.

No one had a better reason than Booker not to trust her.

"I killed fifty of your men with the serum I created. I couldn't ask you for help."

"We've been through this. I don't hold you responsible, Doc. I never did," Booker snapped, then caught her hand in his fingers. He leaned down until his face was mere inches from hers. "You won't believe that."

She still didn't. Not enough to stay with him. Trust him. Love him. Too much history, too many deaths lay between them.

It had been a year since she walked out. A year and two months, she corrected.

He'd changed since then. Leaner than she remembered. Timber-wolf lean, with shaggy brown hair that curled slightly over his back collar.

His face was the same, the cobalt eyes set beneath a high forehead, framed by the broad sweep of his cheekbones, and the hard lines of his jaw and mouth.

"Trygg's on his way," she said, then tugged her hand free. "Maybe if we wait. Catch him unaware. We could stop this all now."

"I'll stop it. But not with you around," he stated,

his tone now brisk, businesslike. "You're going back to the palace."

Muffled gunfire ripped through the night air, moving closer.

"Company's coming." Booker stood, his body unyielding, ready. Almost as if he welcomed the confrontation. He stepped to the window, peered through the two-inch gap between the curtains. Tires screeched on the street below. "A sedan. Four men."

Doors slammed; men yelled orders.

"They'll have the exits covered." In two strides he was back at her side and he pulled her to her feet.

The streetlights glared through the window. She grabbed his arm, pointed at the long shadowy bars that crisscrossed outside the window. "A fire escape."

"All right. Let's go," he said, checking the street again. "It's clear." He slid the window up.

"Wait! My medical bag." She snagged it from the couch, slung the strap crossways from shoulder to opposite hip.

His eyes narrowed on the bag for a quick moment before shifting to her face. "Ready?"

"Yes," she answered, her grip tight on the strap.

Booker pointed the machine gun at the street, then stepped out onto the wrought-iron platform.

Bullets strafed the wall above their heads, shattered the window, pelted the cement behind them.

Booker fired, heard the screams, then the silence.

"Stay close!" They flew down the steps, stumbled past the dead men, one on the ground, the other hung over the stair railing. Their eyes open, sightless.

Booker glanced at the one by his feet, noted the blood-soaked fatigues. "Another of Trygg's mercenaries."

"Not this one," Sandra whispered, indicating the dark-suited man on the railing.

He grabbed the man's face, tilted it toward the streetlamp, then swore.

"Do you know him?"

"Yes. He's one of King Jarek's." Booker shoved the man away. "Follow me. My car is down the street."

Booker stepped down a nearby alley, his gun raised, his focus on the shadows.

At the mouth of the alley, he stopped.

"What?" She peered around him, saw the SUV riddled with bullet holes. "How did they know it was your vehicle?"

"It's a palace car. Jarek's man must have recognized it." He shoved the pistol into the back of his waistband.

"Let's go!" He pulled her behind the SUV and popped the rear hatch. "Keep a lookout."

He grabbed a backpack from the seat.

"I hope you have some artillery in there," she

quipped. The wind picked up, sending shivers down her arms. She hugged her chest. "Or warm clothes."

"No clothes." He slammed the hatch closed. "But I have these." He held out three silver discs. "They'll create a hell of a bonfire."

"Very funny."

"Not joking." He shoved the explosive back into the bag and slung the strap over his shoulder. "Let's keep moving. We need transportation."

One block became three, then six. Her side protested, cramping, squeezing the oxygen from her lungs. When she stopped, Booker suddenly appeared beside her, grabbed her arm and pulled her along.

She stumbled against him, gripped the back of his shirt for balance. "I thought I was in good shape."

"You were tied to a chair for ten hours." Booker stopped midstep. "Look."

A car pulled up across the street. Streamlined, small and sporty. Fire-engine red. A flag of defiance against the opaque browns of the desert city.

"How about that," Booker murmured, a grim smile tugging at his mouth.

"What?" she asked, frowning.

"Our ride just arrived."

Chapter Three

"We traced Sandra's whereabouts to an old apartment building at the south edge of the city." Quamar Bazan turned from the window and addressed his cousin, King Jarek Al Asadi. "We found six men, dead. But did not find Sandra."

Quamar was a giant of a man, with a bald head, darkened features and substantial muscle. "Five mercenaries." He paused, frowning. "And one of our own men."

"What the hell was our man doing there?" Jarek asked. Leaner and just a few inches shorter, he shared his cousin's hard jawline, the same keen brown eyes.

The same fear for Sandra's safety.

"I am not sure. But it appears he wasn't there to help Sandra," Quamar replied, and crossed to the desk.

Jarek's office had changed little over the years. Deep reds and indigo blues patterned the thick carpet, the velvet drapes. Mahogany, scarred from decades of service, gleamed bright with polish. Its lemon scent still strong from the previous morning's cleaning.

"Omar Haddad is performing the autopsies." Quamar rolled his shoulders, stretched the fatigue from the muscles. Tired from the night of searching, he would not sleep until they located Sandra. "The bullets do not seem to match any guns left on the scene."

"Is that a good idea? Having Sandra's father perform the autopsies?"

"It is his duty as acting Royal Physician and Coroner, now that Sandra is missing."

Both men knew the two families' relationship went much deeper than royals and subjects. Omar Haddad was their uncle, if not in blood, in respect and love.

"He insisted," Quamar stated. "And he will be thorough."

"Did you recognize any of them?"

"No. Most likely the remaining five are foreign," Quamar stated flatly, his frustration barely contained. Quamar kept tabs on the less savory in Taer. It bothered him that he did not know these men. "I'm having them run through Interpol."

"No witnesses?"

"One, possibly," Quamar admitted. He poured himself a cup of coffee from a nearby serving cart. A taste he had acquired several years before while working as an operative for Labyrinth—a branch of America's CIA. Black Ops. "Three hours ago, a car was reported stolen. The owner stated a couple forced him from his car. The woman matched the description of Sandra."

He raised the cup, offering it to his cousin.

Jarek waved it off. "And the man?"

"The owner heard the woman call him Booker."

"McKnight?" Jarek straightened, his spine rigid. "How in the hell did he get involved in this?"

"From the pile of dead bodies in the building, it looked more like he saved her," Quamar corrected. "Not just from the foreigners but from our man, as well."

He downed half the hot liquid in one long pull. Strong, it bit at the back of his throat before settling warm in his gut. He topped off the cup one more time, then turned back to his cousin.

"If he has her, why isn't she at the palace? Why didn't Booker bring her directly back here to me?"

"I am trying to find out." Quamar ignored the arrogance of his cousin's demand, knowing it came from concern.

"Omar and Elizabeth are asking for updates on Sandra's situation."

"Tell them she's in good hands."

Quamar raised a brow. "Lie to them?"

"You're the one who said Booker's protecting her," Jarek retorted.

"I said that it appeared Booker saved her—"

"Damn it, Quamar. I won't have them more worried than they already are—"

A knock at the office door stopped Jarek. He glanced at the grandfather clock in the corner of his office. Three in the morning. Jarek raised an eyebrow at Quamar.

The giant shrugged and stepped over to the desk, forming a formidible barrier against the unwelcomed interruption.

"Come in, Trizal," Jarek commanded, his tone neutral, his temper curbed for the moment.

Jarek's secretary stopped just inside the doorway. Once tall, his thin, willowy frame was now slightly bent with age. His hawkish features now more sullen, the bones more predominant. But his hand remained firm on the door handle, his stern and strong voice familiar with its no-nonsense tone that sent many of the palace staff scurrying in fear. "I'm sorry for the interruption, Your Majesty, but you have unexpected visitors. Considering the urgency of Dr. Sandra's disappearance—"

"He'll see me." Cain MacAlister, the current director of Labyrinth, brushed past the royal secretary and into the private office.

The servant nodded stiffly, then turned to Jarek.

"Your Majesty?" His words dripped with indignation, his question quite clear. If Jarek ordered so, the secretary would have thrown Cain MacAlister out on his ear.

And Jarek knew he'd do it without help and with a great deal of pleasure.

"Thank you, Trizal. Please see that a suite is made ready for the director."

"As you wish, Your Majesty." Trizal didn't flicker one glance in the visitor's direction, but instead shut the door behind him with an efficient snap.

"I don't think he likes me, Your Majesty," Cain mused, then shook Jarek's hand.

"Sometimes, I don't like you, Cain," Jarek responded wryly, noting the director hadn't changed since the last time they'd seen each other in D.C. six months earlier. More silver maybe in the jet-black hair, but the steel eyes were sharp, steady. "Since our countries are on good terms, I feel I must tolerate you at best."

Cain chuckled, then turned toward Quamar. "Hello, friend."

"Hello." Quamar pulled the American into a short hug. Both men had become friends while working as Labyrinth operatives years before. "You heard about Sandra?"

"Yes." Cain stepped away and frowned. "Why in the hell did you let her walk out of here?"

"There's a difference between walking and sneaking," Jarek replied. "Her choice to leave was unexpected."

"Have you found her?"

"No." Jarek indicated two high-back leather chairs in front of his desk. "Have you captured Trygg?"

"No. But Intel has him on his way here," Cain answered as they settled into their seats.

"When?"

"Our time, 0600 hours. Yours, 1500."

"Twelve hours ago," Quamar commented. "So he is already here."

"I didn't hear about the breach through the normal channels. It took time to verify my source."

"What source?" Jarek leaned forward, his hand flat on the desk. Self-control was taught to kings at a young age. It took forty years of practice to keep his fist from pounding the desk.

"One of the guards, a Sergeant Thomas Levi, survived the escape," Cain explained. "Chest wound. Just missed his heart. I had to wait until he got out of surgery to verify what happened."

"President Mercer informed me that Trygg escaped while being transported from Leavenworth," Jarek said. "Why was Trygg being transported in the first place?"

"We don't know," Cain managed, the anger, the frustration cutting off each syllable. "The orders to transfer Trygg disappeared. We're tracking them down."

"A federal prisoner transfer just doesn't materialize out of nowhere, Cain," Jarek snapped, and this time he couldn't stop his hand from hitting the desk.

"It comes from the top. And it always leaves a trail of red tape."

"If this one did, we'll find it. You have my word," Cain replied, his body rigid, his tone more so.

"I'm not worried that you and Jon Mercer won't find your traitor, or Trygg," Jarek countered. He'd known President Mercer for years. They'd worked together developing and maintaining Taer's oil trade with the United States. "I'm worried you won't find them in time to save Sandra."

"We're running a check on the men who kidnapped Sandra against Interpol's most-wanted list right now," Quamar stated.

"You have someone in custody?" Cain asked.

"I found several men dead in a room on the outskirts of the city," Quamar answered grimly. "We have a witness who placed her there."

"So where is she now?" Cain questioned.

"We believe Booker McKnight killed the men, then disappeared with Sandra," Jarek added. "We haven't figured out the 'why' yet."

"Booker?" Cain sat back in his chair and crossed his legs.

"You don't sound surprised," Jarek observed.

"Because it makes sense," Cain surmised. "This mess started several years ago on a research project called CIRCADIAN. And it involved both Sandra and Booker."

"We know very little of CIRCADIAN," Quamar

said. "Only that Sandra's involvement made her the main witness at General Trygg's trial. After, when she came home, we took responsibility for her personal safety."

"It was suspected he hadn't given up his quest for CIRCADIAN. And he had many fanatical followers." Jarek settled back into his seat, his fingers locked across his lap. "But what does this have to do with Booker?"

"Sandra discovered, with CIRCADIAN, a possible way for individual cells to be treated and healed at an accelerated rate. With the help of nanite technology."

"Nanites?" Jarek frowned.

"Miniscule sensory vessels, no more than a nanometer in size and composed of carbon," Cain explained. "These particular nanites were made specifically to have a compatible, yet invasive, accessibility to the human body."

"How accelerated?" Jarek asked, his frown deepening.

"Twenty-four hours. Hence CIRCADIAN. It's Latin for consecutive twenty-four hours." Cain reached over and grabbed his briefcase. "The nanites are inhaled, flushed into the bloodstream through the lungs and delivered directly to the injured or sick cells through hundreds of DNA programmed sensors that blanket the carbon. Given the nanites are smaller than a single cell, they can treat each cell individually."

He thumbed the combination on the briefcase lock and popped open the lid. "Treated with the serum, most humans with an illness or injury healed at supernatural speeds. It was a viable concept," he explained, then pulled out a thick manila envelope and handed it to Jarek. "Within the first year of research, Trygg heard about it and used his clout to be the military liaison on the project."

Jarek opened the file and glanced over its contents. "These are Sandra's research notes."

"I thought they were destroyed," Quamar inserted.

"We very rarely destroy files. Especially the projects that show promise," Cain replied wryly. "We just let people believe they're destroyed."

"So Sandra was close," Jarek commented, his eyes still on the documents. "How does that help us now?"

"CIRCADIAN falls in the scope of the Super Soldier image that Trygg was known to promote," Cain clarified. "Heal a soldier faster. Get him back out in the field."

"Kate was originally assigned as the lead on the research."

"Kate?" Quamar asked. Kate MacAlister-D'Amato was the head of the Labyrinth Technology division and a leading scientist in antimatter energy.

She was also Cain's sister, and a good friend of Quamar's.

Cain nodded. "President Mercer's idea. But within a few months Kate and Trygg clashed. Mercer pulled Kate and Trygg brought in another nanite specialist and made Sandra the team leader. She worked tirelessly for the general. Eventually he found her a private lab and isolated her from the outside world. Including his superiors."

Jarek glanced at Cain, surprised. "You're saying she was a prisoner?"

"No. She loved her work," Cain corrected. "And she worked for two years, pouring her soul into the research. But in the end, the results were unsuccessful. The serum attacked healthy tissue at an accelerated rate, damaging internal organs until they hemorrhaged."

"A painful death," Quamar commented, his brow furrowed.

"Yes," Cain agreed. "Sandra tried for months but she couldn't find a way to correct the problem. Eventually, word came down from the Hill that Mercer wanted the project shut down. The serum posed too much of a threat as a weapon of mass destruction."

"And Trygg?" Jarek asked him.

"Trygg disagreed with Mercer," Cain answered. "He believed CIRCADIAN needed more funding."

"When Mercer refused, Trygg stole the formula?" Jarek prompted.

"No," Cain replied. "He didn't need the formula, he had Sandra's loyalty by then. What he needed was money to finance further research."

"He had lost his American backing."

"Exactly," Cain explained. "Trygg understood marketing CIRCADIAN as a weapon would prove profitable. Enough that he could stake more research on correcting the formula."

"But Sandra stopped Trygg," Quamar stated.

"Dead," Cain replied solemnly. "Trygg is driven by his ego. Sandra worshipped the man. But toward the end of the research he made a major tactical error. His ego got in the way. He decided her hero worship would make her an easy recruit into his Super Soldier project. When he approached her, Sandra played along, but secretly started gathering evidence to expose Trygg. At the end, she broke into Trygg's office, downloaded his computer files with all his records and turned him in to the military authorities. And months later, testified against him."

"Who was the nanite specialist Trygg brought in?" Quamar asked.

Jarek glanced at the file. "Doctor Lewis Pitman."

"The records couldn't prove his involvement," Cain advised. "Pitman disappeared from the grid soon after the charges were dropped. We haven't found him yet."

"So what does all of this have to do with Booker?" Jarek returned to the original question.

"Read the last few pages of the report," Cain answered. "By the time Sandra blew the whistle on Trygg, he'd already released CIRCADIAN on a test group days before. She didn't know it at the time."

Jarek flipped through the pages until he found the information. "It says here that Trygg kept the exercise a secret."

"We believe Trygg had started suspecting Sandra's behavior and kept the experiment from her."

Jarek read a little further, then swore. He glanced up at Cain. "Booker's men?"

"This was a whole new biochemical weapon that nobody had heard of before. Trygg needed proof for CIRCADIAN to be marketable," Cain explained. "He decided on human guinea pigs. So he sent several of his military units out on maneuvers at one of our abandoned military bases. Although they couldn't prove it, I think Lewis Pitman dumped the nanites from a plane. A million little micro bugs floating in the air. Fifty men died that day. Most were Booker's troops."

"A death sentence," Quamar muttered, his fist tight. "How did Booker survive?"

"The report says Booker was called away on another assignment right before," Jarek answered for Cain. "He hadn't been on the base."

"The story gets worse," Cain said, his voice grim. "Trygg managed to appear concerned enough to visit each of the men while they fought for their life. He caught the effects of the biochemical reaction on a hidden video camera. Along with the doctor's reports."

"Documenting the result for his buyers," Quamar stated, disgusted. "I have known many men like Trygg. Who feed off of human suffering."

"None of Booker's men survived?" Jarek asked.

"None. CIRCADIAN has no known antidote," Cain answered. "Trygg told Sandra of the deaths while he was being arrested. I know—I was there. She held it together until the guards took him away. Then she collapsed."

"Booker will not let Trygg remain free. He'll kill him first," Jarek acknowledged. He stood, walked over to the window. In an hour or so, the sun would break across the horizon, a warm gold over the pitch and curves of the centuries-old city roofs.

Through the years, he'd lost family. Quamar's mother, and his own father and mother had been murdered. The thought of losing his people at the hands of a madman cut just as deep. "Hell, I would do the same."

"We all would," Cain added.

They'd all spent years in the field. They'd all been responsible for men who never returned home, for families and strangers who got killed, simply because they were in the wrong place, at the wrong time.

"After Trygg's conviction, Booker resigned from

the military," Cain explained. "I recruited him into Labyrinth on President Mercer's recommendation. A few months later, he volunteered to serve in Taer. Because of his expertise in desert warfare, and his background in oil drilling, I approved his assignment."

"Booker's request was no coincidence, Cain," Quamar inserted, suddenly putting all of the pieces together. "He wanted to be close to Sandra."

"You're right but I didn't realize it at the time," Cain agreed. "After the Al Asheera tried to stage that coup on Taer a few years ago, I ordered Booker home to the States and instead, he resigned."

"He said he needed a change of pace," Jarek remembered. "So I kept him on."

"He must have anticipated Trygg's escape," Cain speculated. "Or wanted to keep an eye on Sandra."

"Or both," Jarek inserted.

"Trygg planned his freedom for five years," Quamar reasoned. "To him, freedom without power and respect is a poor existence. For both, he will need to obtain the formula from Sandra, then eliminate her. Booker understands this."

"If Booker wants Trygg, he'd make sure Trygg came to him," Cain added. "That's what we'd all do."

"And there is no better way to do that than to stick close to the one thing Trygg wants," Jarek agreed. "The only thing that would bring him out of hiding."

"Sandra," Cain stated. "She's Booker's bait."

Chapter Four

"Was that necessary?" Sandra demanded. "Hijacking the man's car and leaving him sprawled in the street?"

"You're right, maybe I should've shot him," Booker quipped, then pushed his foot farther down on the accelerator.

"Very funny." She shifted, then winced. Bruises tattooed her arms, blackened her wrists. She reached into her bag, pulled out a few aspirin.

"Are you okay?"

"I'll live." She swallowed the aspirin dry. "Which is more than I could have said six hours ago."

Run-down and empty streets flew past them. Sandra could see the railroad tracks, the warehouses and the Sahara that lay just beyond.

"You're driving us into the desert," she commented, frowning.

"Change of plans," Booker responded. "We're not going back to the palace."

"Because of Jarek's dead guard back there?"

"I hired him several months ago. American. Ex-military. Impeccable record and references. Top security clearance. All of them checked out," Booker admitted, his neck muscles rigid with anger. "If Trygg can get to him, he can get to others."

"You said you hired Jarek's man. Are you still working for Jarek, then? As his head of security?" Sandra asked quietly. She hadn't seen him in months. Hadn't talked to him in a year.

"I'm guessing not anymore." He downshifted, dodged some loose brush and then glanced at the rearview mirror. "I was in a meeting with the Prime Minister of England, Jordan Beck. We were planning his family's visit to Taer when I got word you were taken."

"I was flying to Tourlay when Trygg's men took me."

"Tourlay's a border town filled with lowlifes," Booker stated. "What the hell were you doing traveling there?"

Sandra sighed. "I have…friends in Tourlay who can help me stop Trygg."

"Friends?" Booker commented, annoyed that she'd turn to someone else for help.

"Actually, they are ex-rebels."

"By rebels, you mean Al Asheera rebels?"

She nodded. "For the past year, I've been smuggling medicine and other supplies to their camps," she explained. "They live in poverty, Booker. The men are afraid to work for fear of arrest. The women and children starve."

"Is Jarek aware of your charity work?"

"No. And neither are my parents," she admitted. "They would forbid it simply because I'm putting myself at risk. But it's my choice. It's not Jarek's— or my father's decision."

Booker understood the anger, the bitterness.

Sandra's father, Doctor Omar Haddad—at one time, a world-renowned genetic research scientist— didn't approve of the choices she'd made in her life. Her schooling. Her career. Her decision to return to Taer years before.

"Your parents will be sick with worry, Doc."

Sandra gazed out the window. Streetlamps cast a jaundiced glow against the shadowy buildings.

"My parents will be safer without me around."

An engine gunned behind them. Booker swore, his eyes focused on the rearview mirror, his grip locked on the steering wheel. "Hold on!"

A sedan darted around a corner, slammed into their back bumper. Sandra flew forward, hit the dash with her shoulder. She gripped the dashboard, then swung around, saw the car.

Two Caucasian men. The one in the passenger seat shifted halfway out the window and pointed a machine gun at their car.

"Gun, Booker!"

He slammed on the brake, jerked the steering wheel left and sent the car skidding around the nearest corner.

The sedan whipped around the corner behind them, its tires screeching.

Booker hit the gas, broke free of the city and headed out to the desert.

He glanced at the dashboard gauges. "Let's see what this baby can do."

He swerved off the road onto the sandy plains. Brush banged against the hood, scraped the underbelly and shook the frame until Sandra's teeth rattled.

"Hold on." He spotted the ravine between two sand dunes in the distance.

Sandra followed his eyes. "Going fast in a narrow space might not be the best idea."

Booker cut the wheel into a tight turn and headed straight into the ravine. "If you have a better one, now would be the time to share it."

The sedan turned off the road, following them.

"Where's your gun?" Sandra lowered the passenger window. Wind slapped at her face, kicked grit and dust into the car. "I can stop them with a few well-placed bullets."

"There is no way you are going to shoot at them hanging out the damn window!"

"It's my better idea." She held out her hand. "Give me your pistol."

"Killing people goes against the Hippocratic oath."

"I don't have to shoot them. I can take out their tires."

"Not today." Even if she could, it would only increase the chance she'd get shot or thrown from the vehicle.

Their car hit a rut, slammed them both back in their seats. Booker forced the car onto a flat path, hugged the right side of the ravine.

"Switch with me!" he ordered, then unsnapped his seat belt.

"What?"

"You're small. Unbuckle, and scoot over." He pushed the seat back as far as it could go. "Then place your right foot on the accelerator.

"Of all the stupid…" she muttered. "My shooting them would be easier than this." Still, she unsnapped her seat belt.

Gritting his teeth, he hooked one arm around her back and lifted her onto his thighs. "Put your foot on the gas, and your hands on the steering wheel."

"Got it."

Dodging the steering wheel, she wiggled down between his thighs.

"Okay," she breathed, her knuckles white, her eyes focused on the landscape.

He slid out from under her, ignoring the jab of the middle console, then maneuvered to the other seat. "Keep clear of the brush and walls. I don't want to dodge anything but bullets, got me?" he ordered, his harsh voice cutting across the air rushing through the open passenger window.

Gunfire pelted their back window, shattering the glass.

SANDRA DIDN'T SCREAM. Instead she hit the gas.

"Hold on!" She swerved the car, barely missing twin boulders. Booker grabbed the window frame.

"What the hell are you doing?"

"Trying to keep us alive. This ravine is like a minefield."

"Just keep this damn thing steady and ahead of them. Without pitching me out the window." He aimed his pistol through the back window and emptied the clip into the other car's windshield.

The driver slumped forward. The car skidded, hit the wall, then flipped on its back. Spinning. Once, twice. Its belly burst into flames.

"Hit the accelerator. We just created a bonfire for all their friends to see." Booker turned back and settled in the passenger seat. "Not bad, Doc. Not bad at all."

"Thanks." But a fear was there, one that creased her forehead. "I think."

"Drive back to the road." He glanced at the gas gauge. Full. Perfect. "Then head east."

"East?" Sandra asked, suspicious. "Why?"

"We need a place to lie low for a while," Booker replied.

"What place?"

"Omasto." He leaned his head back against the seat and closed his eyes. "Don't worry, Doc, you'll fit right in."

"And why is that?"

"Your friends the Al Asheera might be there."

TRYGG SHOVED HIS FOOT against the nearest of the two dead men. Years of self-restraint made him hold back the disgust that threatened to let loose.

These men were lucky McKnight killed them. Trygg would've done much worse had they survived without Sandra Haddad in hand.

At his sentencing, the judge told him he wasn't God. But the judge was wrong. They were all wrong.

On the battlefield, he was God. And the men who'd serve him would be indestructible.

Archangels.

Colonel Jim Rayo took the nearest man's chin and tilted it until he could see his features. "Can't be dead more than a few hours, General."

Trygg glanced at the second body, badly burned by the car fire. "How about the others from the apartment? Are they also dead?"

"Yes, sir," Jim replied, frowning. "One man at the apartment was King Jarek's. If McKnight killed him, he'll suspect we have others in the palace." Jim stood and grimly faced the open desert.

"What's on your mind, Jim?"

"Booker McKnight is a top military man. He just killed nine of our men and took Sandra Haddad."

"They weren't our best men. We chose these men specifically. We wanted her to escape. We need her to retrieve the cylinders."

"Yes, sir," Jim responded slowly, knowing he was walking a minefield. "But we still may have underestimated Booker McKnight."

"You might be right," Trygg said after a moment. "I want you to inform our Al Asheera allies that there is a bounty of one million dollars on Sandra Haddad. Alive. Another million on McKnight. Dead." Trygg walked beside him and slapped his shoulder. "Let's keep the pressure on."

But the uneasiness didn't shake itself from between Jim's shoulders. He understood Booker's grief, his drive to find the men responsible. Glancing back, he found the general studying him.

"Everything okay, Colonel?"

"Yes, sir," Jim answered in a short, clipped tone. His jaw tight, his features carefully blank.

The general's strategies had never failed them.

Yet, came the whispered thought.

"Let me know if anything changes, Colonel."

Understanding Booker's grief didn't change twenty years of loyalty to Trygg.

"I will, sir."

ALMOST IMMEDIATELY SANDRA'S adrenaline wore off. Her eyes blinked with fatigue while Booker drove through the night in relative silence. Sandra eventually pushed her seat back and slept.

Dawn broke over the horizon a few hours later. The heat of the morning sun drove up the temperature.

Booker clicked on the air conditioner, felt immediate relief.

They were at less then a quarter of a tank, but only twenty miles from the settlement of Omasto.

Most desert towns were little more than encampments of canvas tents and stick. Some, the more permanent residents, made their homes of stone and animal skins.

Many only stopped to rest, drink water, buy food or fuel. Most used the settlement for trade. Cloth, spices and cookware crowded makeshift tables, spilled over onto blankets covering the sand.

But there were a few, the more corrupt, who bartered in the shadows. Their wares of weapons turned a larger profit out of the hot sun. Away from the inquisitive, the talkative.

Booker needed the latter if he were to keep Sandra safe.

And he knew the man who'd deal with him. The same man who'd tipped him off about her kidnapping. Aaron Sabra. Ex-con. Black-market dealer.

Sandra shifted; her breath deepened.

He'd watched her sleep a hundred times, tangled in the comforter and sheets. Most times, he kissed her awake until the comforter slipped to the floor and tangled limbs took its place.

Now a silk curtain of hair covered part of her face. The dark strands were stark against her pale skin, deepening the shadows beneath her eyes.

Sleep softened the stubborn chin, the feminine pride. Left the vulnerability bare in the soft, delicate lines of her face.

For a moment he ignored the sand, the danger.

The responsibility to his deceased wife and his men.

And he remembered the last time he'd seen Sandra exhausted.

Trygg's trial.

Weeks of waiting. Days of testimony. Her humiliation over her gullibility. Her guilt over the deaths.

Still, Sandra sat in the courtroom, chin out, back rigid, her brown eyes wide but leveled. She bared her soul to condemn Trygg's.

When Cain MacAlister insisted she enter witness protection, she refused. But Booker wasn't surprised. Being a doctor meant everything to her.

She wouldn't walk away from it or her family for any reason.

"How far are we out?" Her eyes slowly opened, heavy with sleep.

"Less than twenty miles."

She scooted upright and stretched her shoulders. Her hair tumbled in soft waves around her shoulders. With a careless hand, she pushed it back.

"And then?"

"I take you back to the palace," Booker stated. "Jarek has guards that have been loyal to him through the years. I'll make sure he assigns several to you."

"And my family?"

"If we need to."

"Trygg wants my formula, Booker," Sandra said almost sadly. "He wants CIRCADIAN. And he won't let anyone stop him from getting it."

"I thought the government destroyed everything related to project CIRCADIAN. Including the formula and research notes."

"I took four cylinders of the serum before I turned in Trygg." Sandra sighed. She rubbed the knot of tension from the back of her neck, felt a spot of dried blood at the hairline. From her skirmish at the airport, she was sure. "I hid them in the mountain near Tourlay for safekeeping."

For a moment Booker said nothing, but the muscle

on his jaw worked overtime. "This is the real reason you left me, isn't it? To protect your serum."

Sandra stiffened against the sting of his words. "That's not true."

"Think about it," Booker replied. "I've always said I trusted you. But you decided that once your secret was out, I really wouldn't trust you. And I'd be the one to walk away. So you walked first."

Something in his words hit a chord deep within her. Was he right? Was it her defense mechanism against Booker?

She shook her head, pushing the thought away. "I was protecting my research."

"You were protecting a biochemical weapon."

"It isn't a weapon," she argued. "I took the serum because my research wasn't completed. I hadn't found the solution to advance a subject's healing."

"You can't bring my men back, Doc."

"But I might have been able to save others, if I'd been able to complete my research," she stated. "I couldn't tell you any of this, Booker, not without involving you further."

When he raised an eyebrow, she crossed her arms. "It's the truth, damn it."

"Well, I'm involved now." Booker's jaw tightened. "Trygg released one cylinder on my men. What would he do with four?"

"Two is enough to take out a small country."

"Like Taer."

"Yes."

"Given the opportunity, you think Trygg will destroy your country for revenge?"

"You know he will."

"Yes," Booker admitted, then swore. "Trygg is strictly about the bottom line, but it's driven by ego. Everything he does moves him closer to one end."

"The Super Soldier," Sandra acknowledged.

"With an army like that, he can win any war. Does he know about the four cylinders?"

"I didn't think so. But now I'm not so sure," she admitted. "That's why we need to get them."

"And destroy them," Booker added.

"Yes," she agreed, for the moment. She needed time to really think that step through before deciding.

Booker parked the car in front of a small hutted mercantile. His eyes scanned the perimeter, focused on the people moving about.

Women mostly, some watching their children play. Others napping with the smaller ones under makeshift lean-tos.

He took out his pistol, checked the clip. "I want you to stay in the car, Doc. Until I'm sure it's safe."

"No," Sandra answered, more worried about the anger set in his granite features than her own safety. Booker might have spent most of his career walking into hostile situations, but she refused to believe these people were hostile.

"I've traveled here on my own." She shoved the door open. The air was thin and brittle with the heat. It sucked what little moisture she had from her pores. "These people are mostly women and children. They have nothing to do with Trygg."

"More friends of yours?"

"Look, McKnight. I'm tired, I'm hungry and I have a full bladder," she said defensively. They'd driven all morning, only taking a break to relieve themselves. "You do not want to mess with me right now."

He caught her hand before she stepped out of the car. Sandra's chest tightened. His fingers interlocked with hers, squeezing gently.

She'd forgotten how it felt, the intimacy, the simple slide of skin on skin. Without thinking, she gripped his hand back.

"This is not a game, Doc," Booker reminded her.

Maybe it was the low and even tone of his voice, the touch of his fingers, the fact he tilted her chin up until their eyes locked.

The familiarity of all three.

"Considering what I've been living with these past six years, I'm more aware of that than you might think," Sandra pointed out softly.

"You're not the only one who has been living with it," Booker murmured, but his fingers tightened on hers to soften the reminder.

Sadness swept over her. "I know." She breathed out the words. "And I am sorry."

Something broke loose inside her, something she'd held back for almost a year.

"You protect. I heal, Booker." She touched a finger to the lock of hair on his forehead. Then brushed it back, testing his limits. "Let me try to do my job."

When he didn't move, she leaned in, then up until their lips almost touched. "Maybe I'll heal us both in the process," she whispered.

With a groan, he pulled her to him. His mouth covered hers, just as she wanted, just as she remembered.

Desire tumbled free, caught between them, pushed and pulled by longing, need…months of loneliness.

He took, she gave, until the air thickened, the edges of reality blurred.

She'd missed him. Missed this. His arms tightened, drawing her into his lap as if he missed her, too.

Suddenly, Booker broke away, his gun raised behind her back, pointed at the window. "That's a good way to get shot, Sabra."

Sandra jerked around, her heart in overdrive, until realization hit.

Booker hadn't missed her. He'd been protecting her.

Her heart jerked, just a bit.

She shouldn't have been surprised. Or disappointed. But she was. On both counts.

A man stood outside the car, his own gun slowly lowering.

"So is kissing a woman in the middle of nowhere." He stepped back, his gait hindered by a severe limp.

Sandra noted the light brown hair pulled back into a ponytail, the cold black eyes that scanned the horizon behind them, before they rested back on Booker.

"You look like hell, McKnight," the man commented when they stepped out of the car.

Sandra leaned back through the door, and grabbed her medical bag.

"Aaron Sabra," Booker cut in. "Doctor Sandra Haddad."

"Mr. Sabra."

He noticed she didn't offer her hand and smiled. "Aaron works, Doc."

"Doctor Haddad," Booker corrected. Sandra raised an eyebrow but said nothing.

Aaron paused, then nodded once. But his smile widened. "This way, *Doctor Haddad.*

"It's a pleasure to meet you properly," Aaron said when Sandra and Booker joined him. They walked toward the far side of the village. "You've quite a reputation in this part of the country, Doctor."

Surprised, she glanced up at him. "Reputation?"

"Delivering medical supplies, clothes and food to some of the smaller villages. Of course, you're using the Al Asheera, who are my competitors. For the supplies that aren't quite available through more legitimate distributors, I mean."

She ignored Booker's scowl. "You deal in the black market?"

"Among other things," Aaron mused. He led them into a nearby building. The only one, Sandra noted, that had four solid walls and an actual roof.

"It isn't much, but it's home."

It was a sparsely furnished room, no more than ten feet square. A battered desk and chair at one end, a cot at the other. A table and three more chairs in the middle.

Aaron sat down behind his desk and lifted his leg up on a nearby stool.

"I don't have much to offer except maybe some lukewarm coffee." He nodded to a potbellied stove in the corner. On its burner sat a blackened teakettle. "You are welcome to it and whatever else I have at hand."

He gestured to the small wooden table nearby. Some sweetened bread, fruit and cheese filled two plates.

Sandra's stomach growled. She sat in one of the straight-back chairs and sliced a thick piece of the bread, then offered it to Booker.

He shook his head.

"Maybe the doctor would like a change of clothes and somewhere to wash up?" Aaron commented.

"I might." Sandra took a bite of the bread, enjoying the traditional spicy sweetness, even as her eyes remained on the two men. "After I hear how you two know each other."

"Aaron worked at the drilling site for a while," Booker admitted.

"Until I hurt my leg in a rigging accident," Aaron commented. "And realized I preferred desert living to drilling. So I got into supply and demand. Booker and I exchange favors from time to time."

"A necessary relationship. But not always a trusting one," Booker quipped.

Aaron leaned back in his chair, a small smile on his lips, one that didn't quite reach the black of his eyes. "Almost like the two of you, I suspect."

"I doubt it," Sandra scoffed, then remembered the shared kiss in the car. She stood, suddenly needing time alone to think things through. She'd let them hash out the car situation. "Would you have any clean clothes I could add to his tab of favors?"

"Of course," Aaron replied, a grin on his face. "Any friend of Booker's…"

Chapter Five

Aaron found a change of clothes for both Sandra and Booker.

The men stepped outside the mercantile to give her privacy. Without warning, Booker shoved Aaron back against the wall and gripped his throat.

"I want to know how you found out about Trygg's plan to kidnap the doc."

"I hear things," Aaron gasped, but he didn't move. "It goes with my occupation. A friend of a friend of a friend. Someone overhearing a conversation. Sometimes, even as pillow talk."

Booker's grip tightened. "Who told you?"

"One of the mercenaries who took her."

"Why tell me?"

"You think I'd stand by while Trygg kills innocents?" Aaron snapped back. "Killing women and children is not my style. And that goes for your woman. I didn't lie when I said she's got a lot of support from the locals around here. She helped a lot of people, McKnight. Most who'd given up hope for a better life. Any kind of life."

Booker studied his face, then slowly released his grip and stepped back. "She isn't my woman."

"Sure, she isn't. And this isn't a windpipe you almost crushed." Aaron rubbed his throat for a moment. "Number-one rule. Don't make it personal."

"Like you haven't?" He glanced around. "Seems to me, the doc isn't the only one providing shelter and food around here."

Aaron reached into his shirt pocket, withdrew a pack of cigarettes and a lighter. He flipped the lighter open, held the cigarette to the flame, then snapped it shut.

"I met Trygg once in Leavenworth while doing my time, right after he'd been incarcerated," Aaron acknowledged, then took a long drag on the cigarette. "Trygg isn't a sane man. And those following him are fanatically loyal."

"Sometimes it's loyalty." Booker turned on his heel and headed for the well in the middle of the settlement. "And sometimes it just takes putting the right amount of money in the right hands."

Aaron fell into step beside him, blew out a stream of smoke. "Like I said, you are too close to the situation. It has become too personal, my friend."

"I'm not your friend," Booker answered, his words clipped. He hung a clean shirt—an army issued khaki T-shirt—over the well wall and pulled up the bucket from the water.

"And it was never anything but personal."

"You know what I think?" Booker pulled his shirt off and dropped it to the ground. "Maybe you need to find a hobby."

"Or maybe I should fall in love with a woman," Aaron argued, then grinned. Booker hesitated for a split second, enough for Aaron to know his insinuation hit its mark.

"She's a means to an end." Booker splashed the cool water on his face, scratched the whiskers that scraped against his palm. "I had little choice."

Booker splashed more water on his chest and armpits.

"I don't blame you. She's smart. Beautiful. And rich."

Booker grabbed his clean shirt, dried off with it, then put it on. "You keep going and you'll have two limps to deal with, Sabra."

"Love makes things complicated, doesn't it?" Aaron mused, staring at the tip of his cigarette.

"What the hell are you talking about?"

"You are in love with the woman who might be responsible for your wife, Emily's, death."

Booker faced Aaron, his hands fisted. "How the hell did you get ahold of that information?"

"All it takes is putting the right amount of money in the right hands." Aaron repeated Booker's earlier words, his features sharpening. "She doesn't know, does she?"

"No." Booker's eyes narrowed. "And if she finds out—"

"Don't worry. Your secret's safe with me. Over the last few months, I've grown found of Dr. Haddad and what she's done for the desert people. Enough that I don't want to be the bearer of bad news."

"Booker!"

Sandra stepped from the doorway. The sun caught her hair, deepened the black until it shimmered. With quick fingers, she twisted her hair up and secured it in a loose bun. Then wrapped a white linen scarf around her head and neck for protection.

"Men's clothing never looked so good on a woman, has it?" Aaron said.

The light cotton pants and shirt were man-sized. A small man, Booker realized, noting that the clothes fit snug over the hips, and stretched across her derriere.

He clenched his jaw, just for a moment, remembering how his fingers cupped the round curves earlier in the car. His body tightened with need—and frustration.

She made her way to the nearest horse trough. Once there, she adjusted the medical bag back farther on her shoulder, leaned over and washed her hands.

"Doctor Sandra!" Suddenly, a group of children ran toward her. Their mothers followed. Within moments, Sandra was surrounded by many of the villagers. Some hugging her, others showing her an injury or talking rapidly in an attempt to explain—what, Booker didn't know.

It appeared most just wanted to wish her a warm welcome. Sandra hugged the women, then knelt down and hugged the smaller children. The boys and girls too old to hug, she would tug on a lock of hair beneath a scarf or pat them on the head.

"I told you, she is loved by these people whom Taer and its king have forgotten."

"Do you think he has really forgotten? Or just remembers differently?" Booker asked. He had to admit, he'd never seen Sandra so happy.

It seemed to him that when she could not find her place among her own family, she found another out in the desert.

Sandra broke away from the crowd and waved to Booker. "I'll be back in a few minutes. I want to use the outhouse."

"No," Aaron shouted before Booker gave his approval.

"Why?" Booker asked, then watched Sandra start toward them instead.

"I've got two prisoners locked in there. I was just getting ready to question them when you pulled in."

BOOKER SWUNG AROUND, angry. "Prisoners?"

"Two men arrived about an hour ago. They offered

quite a lot of money for the capture of Doctor Haddad. And even more for your dead body."

"How much money?"

"A few million," Aaron answered, then laughed. "I almost considered claiming the reward when I saw you in the car. But after that kiss…well, I do consider myself a romantic at heart, McKnight."

Booker grunted. "Sometimes I wonder which side you're on."

"Right now?" Aaron's mouth twitched. "Her side."

Booker followed the other man's gaze until his own settled on the doc as she approached.

"Then for right now, we're on the same side."

Sandra walked up. "Did I miss something?" She eyed the two men.

"Sabra has two prisoners locked up in the outhouse," Booker said. "They might work for Trygg."

"Wait here," Aaron replied. "I'll have them brought to my office for you to question."

Aaron walked toward two men watering camels by the trough. He waved them over to the outhouse.

"What are you planning?" Sandra asked.

"Sabra said they were offering a high price for our capture," Booker answered, deliberately leaving out the fact Trygg wanted him dead. "I want to ask them a few questions."

"Give my men a few minutes." Aaron leaned against the side of the sports car and crossed his arms. "We can use the time to negotiate my price."

"Price?" Sandra asked, not sure she understood.

Aaron flicked his cigarette away. "I get the sports car."

"You can't be serious," Sandra scoffed. "What happens if the owner comes looking for it?"

"The owner has insurance. The only thing he'll be looking for is a newer model to replace it." Aaron leaned in the window and studied the custom leather seats, the state-of-the-art dashboard. "I'll give you food, water and transportation. Enough to get you across the desert."

"Deal." Booker glanced at the camels taking their fill of water from the trough. "And the transportation better have wheels."

"Whatever you'd like." Aaron smiled, then straightened when one of his men waved them over. "Give me a minute, then follow me in."

Booker waited until Aaron entered the hut, then turned to Sandra. "No matter what happens, Doc, you don't move from this spot until I give you permission."

"I haven't needed permission to do anything for quite a while, McKnight," Sandra snapped. "This is my problem. I will not be left out of it."

"I can't protect you and question them at the same time."

Sandra pulled a pistol from her medical bag. "I don't need your protection. I have my own."

Booker stared at the 9mm Glock in her hand. "Where the hell did you get that?"

"Aaron's desk drawer. I don't usually steal, but I figured he had a warehouse full somewhere." She started toward the hut. After a few moments, she looked back. "Are you coming?"

A gunshot ricocheted through the air. Booker reached for his gun. "Stay here!" he barked.

Before she could answer, he slipped around the corner and into the mercantile.

One of the men was dead on the floor, his pistol still in his hand. Aaron had the other man sitting down in a straight-back chair, a Sig Sauer pointed at his chest.

"The one on the floor had a gun hidden. He tried to shoot me," Aaron said, his features slanted with anger. "I shot first."

Booker recognized the man in the chair. "Kalroy. What brings you so far out from the palace?"

"King Jarek sent me. I tried to tell him that we are on the same side," the man responded, his voice more of a whine than angry. "That I was here to retrieve Doctor Haddad. Is she here?"

"Right behind you," Aaron mused.

"Kalroy." Sarah stepped through the doorway, took in the situation, her gun lowered but in her hand. She glanced at the dead man, noticed the army fatigues.

"He's not Jarek's man, is he?" she asked.

"No," Booker replied. He looked at Kalroy. "Your dead friend on the floor is one of Trygg's mercenaries, isn't he?"

Aaron checked the dead man's pockets. "He has no identification."

"How much did Trygg pay you?" Sandra asked. "To peddle a reward for my capture?"

Kalroy shook his head. "I have no idea what you are talking about."

Booker dropped the barrel of his gun to Kalroy's left knee and fired.

Kalroy screamed. He rolled onto the floor and clutched his knee. Sandra bit her lip but did not say anything.

"Try again," Booker suggested, his tone low, almost guttural.

"Trygg's man, Rayo, paid me six months' salary to bring his man here." Sweat beaded Kalroy's face. Pain etched his features.

"And if you found her?" Booker demanded.

"We were to kill you, and take her to Tourlay. Then collect the reward."

"Where in Tourlay?"

"Only he knew," Kalroy answered, then nodded to the dead man. "I wasn't told."

"All right." Booker shrugged, then lowered his gun. "I believe you—"

Suddenly, Kalroy lunged for the dead man's pistol. Booker fired into the back of the traitor's skull.

"You did that on purpose, didn't you?" Sandra asked. "You knew Kalroy would reach for his gun."

"I'd hoped," Booker said flatly, then looked at Aaron. "You have the sports car. I'm taking their car. Consider us even. You can do whatever you want with the bodies."

Chapter Six

There weren't too many duties Jim Rayo hated.

Acting as delivery boy, however, was at the top of his list.

He parked his jeep at the crest of a nearby dune, and studied the perimeter. The sun hit the top of the sky, turning the Sahara into miles of molten gold.

He'd been here before. Many times over the years. But most of those times, blood stained the sand, clogged the air. And bodies littered the dunes.

He'd followed Riorden Trygg for twenty-five years. A little more than half his life. Desert Storm. Operation Freedom. Several known occupations and others not so known.

Through it all, Trygg had saved his life more than a dozen times, bailed his butt out of bad situations countless more.

When Trygg had first found him, Jim had been barely in his twenties. He'd been tried and convicted for manslaughter after a drunken brawl escalated into a knife fight.

Trygg walked into his cell like he owned Leavenworth. He'd been a colonel back then. His chest crammed with metals, his hair short and tight, a cigar hanging out of his mouth. And a half a dozen more shoved in the shirt pockets of prison guards.

Trygg gave him a choice. Thirty years in prison, or his full rank back and an opportunity to serve his country the way he'd always intended.

The only thing Trygg required was Jim's word. His sworn loyalty.

From that day, he'd followed Trygg throughout numerous countries, campaigns and, finally, to Capitol Hill. Neither man had broken his promise.

He even shared Trygg's goal of creating the perfect soldier.

But all of it had changed with CIRCADIAN.

The whir of a helicopter split the air. Jim watched the bird land several yards away, the pilot giving him the high sign.

Jim waited until a slight, mousy man jumped from the opening. Military gear hung on his small frame along with a briefcase strapped over his shoulder and a gray gym bag gripped in one hand.

"Colonel." Doctor Lewis Pitman tossed the gym bag into the back of the jeep and slid onto the passenger seat. "Are we on schedule?"

"Yes." Jim started the vehicle. "We're in the last stages."

"Good. Good," Lewis said. He placed his briefcase at his feet and fastened his seat belt. "And Dr. Haddad? Is she at the camp?"

"No."

Pitman frowned. "If we are in the last stages, we need her within the next forty-eight hours. I need time to adapt my systems. You realize that, right, Colonel?"

"Yes. And so does the general," Jim reminded him. "We expect she'll be joining us within the next twelve hours."

"Joining us?" Pitman sneered. "This isn't a goddamn tea party."

"It isn't your operation, either." Jim's eyes narrowed. "Are we clear?"

"Fine." Lewis backed down, more out of fear than accord, Jim suspected.

"How much farther?"

"It's just over the next hill," Jim replied. "The general is waiting for you at camp to discuss the final plans."

They crested the dune and Lewis let out a long whistle. His eyes moved to an airbus parked at the base of a five-hundred-foot-high rock formation. The plane itself was forty feet high and well over one hundred feet in length, its white body covered in camo clustered netting from tail to nose.

"Well, hello, sexy." Lewis jumped from the jeep the moment Jim parked.

"Dr. Pitman." General Trygg approached from a

nearby tent, caught the smile on the scientist's face. "I can see you're pleased with our efforts."

"General," Lewis answered, then slowly shook his head. "I can't believe you did it. That you pulled it off."

"It's been refit to your specifications." General Trygg stopped, his eyes flickering over the plane. "At great cost to my operation."

"The payoff will quadruple your investment," Pitman assured him. "A moving laboratory will be hard to detect once we disperse the CIRCADIAN."

Trygg glanced at Jim. "Everything go well, Colonel?"

"Yes, sir. The helicopter was on time."

"Colonel Rayo informed me that Sandra Haddad is not here. I must point out that without her—"

"You worry about the nanites, Lewis," the general interrupted. "I will take care of Doctor Haddad."

"I don't think you understand the importance—"

"Listen to me. I will take care of Doctor Haddad."

Jim understood the general well. The emotionless features, the toneless response, the hard set of his shoulders, told him Trygg was just shy of losing his temper.

"Let me show you the airbus, Doctor Pitman." Jim's eyes caught Trygg's. "Go ahead of me. I'll catch up with your bags in a minute."

Trygg gave a sharp nod. "Good idea, Jim."

"All right," Lewis conceded. "I will do my part, and rely on you to do yours."

"Thank you, Lewis," Trygg responded dryly, then watched the doctor head for the plane.

Over the years, Jim had worked with many men and dealt with many personalities. Most, he coped with. But intuition and experience had taught him to quickly identify weaknesses in character. And Lewis Pitman's backbone would break like a toothpick.

"I don't trust him," Jim commented in a low tone. "He'll cut and run at the first sign of trouble."

The general clapped him on the shoulder. "He's already cut and run. Right after I was imprisoned. Remember? A coward doesn't change. He just moves on."

"Why ask Lewis Pitman back on this project?"

"Don't worry," Trygg reassured him. "I don't trust the man, but I trust the fact that a coward stays a coward."

Jim nodded. "Know your enemies. Keep them close."

Trygg watched Pitman climb into the airplane. "He'll make an excellent experimental rat."

"Understood." Jim had no sympathy for the man. Over the course of the years, he had eradicated many of the same.

"Now—" Trygg's lips moved into a genuine smile "—I smelled coffee earlier coming from the mess tent. Why don't I buy you a cup and you can give me a situation report?"

"I have to skip the coffee, sir. We're missing two more men," Jim answered, and walked with the general to the tent across their base. "The messengers I sent to get word out on our rewards for Doctor Haddad and McKnight."

"Where is the good doctor?"

"East of us. Somewhere past Omasto."

Trygg frowned. "That doesn't bode well. Tourlay lies farther north. I know those cylinders are there. Or nearby. Otherwise she wouldn't have booked her flight there."

"Yes, sir," the colonel responded. "I'm sending some men out in the helicopter."

"I'll show Lewis the laboratory. I want you to monitor your men and then report back when you get done," Trygg ordered. "We need those cylinders in the next twelve hours."

"And McKnight? If we take her, should we keep him alive for insurance?"

"No. Keeping McKnight alive is too much of a risk. If it comes to that, it's best to kill him on sight. We simply find more painful ways of getting Haddad to break."

Jim's stomach tightened. Torturing a woman wasn't in his nature. And it was highly likely, given Sandra Haddad's personality, she'd die before revealing the location of the cylinders.

Rayo pushed the image of that out of his mind to focus on a question that had been nagging at him for the past few weeks.

"Can I ask where you've gotten this intel from, sir?"

"A close friend."

"In Washington?" Jim pressed.

Trygg laughed, then slapped Jim on the shoulder. But the fingers stayed, dug in just enough to pinch the nerve. "I could tell you, but then I'd have to kill you."

"ALL RIGHT, DOC," Booker demanded. "Tell me exactly where those cylinders are hidden."

The sun had set an hour earlier. They'd been driving for nearly two hours in unsettled silence. The soft green glow of the dashboard edged the darkness, filling the car with an eerie expectancy.

"They're in a cave. The landscape might have changed some of my landmarks. It might take a while to find them again," Sandra explained. "That's why it's essential I go with you."

She dropped her head back against the seat and closed her eyes. "I almost had it, Booker."

"Had what?"

She opened her eyes. "The answer." She held up her hand, brought her finger and thumb within a centimeter of each other. "I was this close to figuring out the problem with my formula. I couldn't walk away from years of research and experiments. This wasn't about ego or Trygg's Super Soldier dream. This was about making sick people well."

She dropped her hand into her lap, tightened the fingers into a fist. "When they confiscated my files, something snapped in me. Something ugly."

"And you took the cylinders."

"When I came to my senses, it was too late to return them, and I couldn't destroy them myself. So I buried them in a cave."

"It never occurred to you that Trygg discovered your secret?"

She shook her head. "I took them the same day Cain arrested him," she explained. "There was only one person who could have known. And I thought he was long gone."

"Lewis Pitman."

"Yes. He worked closely with me on the experiments." She stiffened in surprise. "How did you know about Pitman?"

"Let's just say I've had a long time to do my research on the CIRCADIAN project."

"Including some hands-on research with me," she reasoned, struggling to keep the sudden surge of humiliation and anger in check.

"What are you talking about, Doc?"

"Our last night together, when I confessed my involvement with the deaths of your men, you already knew about it."

"I'd known since the trial."

"Our meeting was no accident then," she said slowly. "You understood Trygg would come after me if he had the chance."

"Yes, I figured you might be a target if he ever escaped prison. But I didn't know about your close relationship with the royals or the fact that our paths would cross often once I started working for Jarek." Booker sighed. "While our first meeting wasn't planned, it was inevitable, Doc."

"And after, when we…" She was unable to go on.

"Slept together?" he supplied. "That had nothing to do with Trygg. Only you and me were in that bed together. No one else." Booker stopped the SUV in front of a small oasis of brush and rocks. He turned off the motor.

"You should have told me, Booker."

"It took you three months to tell me, Doc." He shifted around until he faced her. His elbow rested on the back of the seat and his fingers came dangerously close to her shoulder and hair.

"But I told you immediately after I found out who you were."

"By the time I realized you didn't know, we were heading for more than just a casual relationship. At that point, it didn't make a difference."

"It would have made a difference in me," she countered. "Your knowing might have stopped me from…"

"From what?"

From falling in love with you. "From getting involved with you," she snapped instead.

"That wasn't going to happen." His fingers caught a loop of hair. "Something sparked between us the moment we met."

She couldn't deny it. Quamar had introduced them at one of the many balls held at the palace.

The moment they'd touched hands, something rippled through them, crackled the air around them.

"We can't go back in time, Booker. Too much has happened." She pulled her head away, not liking how each tug on her hair made her pulse jump. "Let's just finish this. Then we both can get on with our lives."

Without warning, the air rushed around them. Booker's head jerked; his eyes narrowed on the darkness. He hit the lights on the jeep. "Listen!"

The soft *whop whop* of blades hit the air.

Booker swore. "Helicopter."

His turned the ignition on, kept the lights off and slammed the gearshift into Drive.

The SUV jerked to life. The tires tore through the sand, sending dirt and dust flying. Booker plowed through brush, then shot over a dune.

The vehicle caught air, hit the bottom of the dune. Sandra screamed. "How did they find us?"

Suddenly, a helicopter rose over the next dune. Its engine eerily silent. Muffled.

Stealth.

Its spotlights glared down on them.

"Stop your vehicle." The order burst from the helicopter's loudspeaker. *"If you do not stop, we will be forced to fire upon you."*

"Hold on to something!" Booker stomped on the brake, slammed the gearshift into Reverse and hit the accelerator.

They sped backward down the hill, swerving and putting the helicopter temporarily out of firing sight.

Machine guns fired. The bullets ripped across the back window of the SUV. The rear window exploded.

"Can this thing fly?" Sandra glanced back, knowing it would be impossible to outrun the chopper for long.

"No. But it can detonate." Booker hit a button on the dashboard. A drawer from beneath opened up. Six silver disks lay in a line. "These are magnetic explosives. Each has a thirty-second delayed trigger."

"This is why you wanted the palace SUV?"

"Yes," he answered. "There's enough explosives in each of those to flatten a small house."

"Then why can't we just throw them at the bad guys?" she demanded, slinging her medical bag over her shoulder. "Out in the desert with nothing but the clothes on our backs is not my idea of a good time, Booker!"

"It's better odds than dealing with them." He pointed at the helicopter once again above them.

Booker stopped the car. "Out! Now!" he ordered.

Sandra shoved the door open and she scrambled out.

He aimed the car toward the belly of the helicopter, threw the car into Drive and stomped on the gas.

Closing on the copter fast, he pressed the triggers on each of the discs, counting off twenty-five seconds in his head. He shoved the door open and jumped.

The explosion hit the night air. The helicopter took the brunt of it in its belly and tail. In a grind of metal it started a death spin.

Booker scrambled to his feet, ignoring the rush of pain in his side. Instead, he searched for Sandra.

A thunderous rumble shook the earth beneath his feet. Booker swore and looked to the horizon.

Horses. Fifty of them clambered over the dunes from all directions. Led by the men on their backs, their swords raised.

"Booker!" Sandra screamed from behind him. He swung around. A horse rose on its hind legs in front of her, its front hooves punching the air mere inches from her head.

Booker scrambled after her. Two men jumped in his path. He punched one in the neck, grabbed the man's rifle and clubbed the other.

"Stay there!" A man, Al Asheera, pointed his rifle at her with one hand while he tried to control the horse with the other.

Booker stopped, aimed and fired. The man stiffened, then slid dead from the horse.

"Come on!" Booker grabbed her arm, hauled her to her feet.

"Where—"

"Not now!" He dragged her across the sand to the horse.

He grabbed the reins, brought the horse around. "Get on!" he ordered. "In front."

Men yelled, catching sight of the couple. Gunfire strafed the sand at their feet. Booker bent over, grabbed her foot and hoisted her in the saddle before settling behind her.

"Hey ya!" he ordered, and hit the horse's ribs with his heels. They shot across the dunes, racing across the desert, letting the darkness swallow them whole.

Chapter Seven

The dark sky softened slowly into the predawn light.

Booker stopped once, taking a few moments to get his bearings and search through the canvas sack attached to the horse's saddle.

The man had left them nothing more than flat bread and cheese, a few containers of water and rifle ammunition.

Sandra slept against his chest, her eyes closed, her face settled into the curve of his neck.

From the moment he'd found out Trygg had taken her, he lived with fear. Fear he wouldn't get to her in time. Fear he couldn't protect her.

Fear that he'd fall in love with her again.

Without thought, Booker's arm tightened around her.

The wind whipped around them, catching her hair, just enough for a few wisps to tickle his cheek.

Booker tapped the horse's sides, picking up its gait.

Sandra shifted closer, her curves soft against his thighs, the tight muscles of his stomach.

His body strained against the intimacy, while the echoes of their earlier conversation went through his mind.

She insisted this was only about Trygg. He knew better.

His hand gripped the reins tighter. Anger was easier. If only she hadn't stolen those cylinders, hadn't made herself a target...Booker never would have met her.

She sighed, snuggled her backside between his thighs. Booker gritted his teeth.

The desire, the need, had been there from the beginning.

The first time they had talked, had touched.

The first time she'd smiled.

When he'd lost his wife, Booker mourned. Dark days of grief, anger—guilt.

It took falling in love with Sandra for him to understand.

He'd never loved Emily like this.

He'd been attracted to her. He loved her spirit, her craving for excitement. Life was her playground and she was the princess.

Once they were married, he'd expected her to slow down, to settle into the marriage. But when she didn't, it caused problems. Her flirting. The partying.

Their fighting escalated until, tired of it, Booker

stayed away from home more often, not wanting to deal with her tantrums.

If he'd paid more attention to her. If she hadn't followed him to the base. But he'd been caught up in his military career. Trying to prove something, make something of himself, at the cost of his marriage.

Emily had come looking for him that day. To tell him she was pregnant.

And inhaled the CIRCADIAN.

Sandra's head shifted back into the hollow of his shoulder, exposing the long line of her neck.

He'd watched Sandra for two years.

The woman who brought Trygg down.

Her habits. He'd bugged her phones, her apartment. She made a move, he followed.

She haunted him. His dreams, his nightmares. Emily's red hair became a dark, rich black. Her blue eyes darkened to a deep mahogany brown.

Soon Emily's features blurred into Sandra's. Stayed Sandra's.

She burrowed in, her breath warm against his skin. Slowly, without thought, Booker held the reins with one hand and slid his palm over her rib cage, just inches from her breast. He felt adolescent, copping a feel, so he forced his hand to stop.

"Sandra, wake up," he whispered, hoarse with restraint.

Her eyes blinked open. Widened at the desire he

didn't hide from his features. The silent question that haunted his eyes.

Her gaze dropped to his mouth. Without a word, she shifted closer until her lips touched his.

Desire—held in check for far too long—broke free. With a groan, he pulled her closer. The rhythm of the horse set a sexy, heated tempo as their bodies bumped, pressed, bumped.

Booker dropped the reins, let the horse have his lead.

Suddenly, Sandra found herself lifted and turned so that her legs straddled his waist. The hard result of their kissing pressed against the apex of her thighs.

His hands slipped under her shirt, slid over her back; his fingers ran up her spine, then down, until each hand gripped a butt cheek and brought her in closer.

They both groaned.

His mouth found hers. His tongue was merciless as it stroked and burned inside her mouth.

Booker tapped the horse with his heels.

The horse stepped into a slow canter. Sandra gasped; her hands gripped his shoulders, felt the muscles flex beneath her palms.

Sandra lost all track of her surroundings. His hands grasped her hips, holding her tight against him while their bodies matched the horse's gait.

Heat pitted in her stomach. Liquid fire flowed between her thighs.

"Booker," she whispered. Her hands slipped behind his head, bringing his mouth to hers. Her fingers shoved the scarf aside, buried themselves in the thickest part of his hair.

His hand delved between her cheeks, felt the wet, soft center of her.

The sun broke free of the horizon. Sandra blinked into its harsh glare.

She pulled back, humiliated. "This won't solve our problems."

Booker shuddered and pulled away. "All right. We'll play it your way," Booker answered, his voice little more than gravel and glass shards.

"Now isn't the time," she said, straightening her shirt. "But our timing has always been off," she acknowledged with a weak smile.

"We're tired," he reasoned, his eyes on the horizon, not her. "We only have a couple more hours before the sun gets too hot for us to continue."

He jabbed a finger at the mountains in the distance. "We should hit the foothills right about the same time. If I have my bearings right, there is an oasis hidden in the crevices at the base."

"Malaquo," Sandra murmured, forcing herself not to rub the ache in her heart. "I know it pretty well."

Unable to sit close to her, he set her forward and

slid off. Deftly, he swung the reins over the horse's head. "Time to give the horse a break."

When Sandra shifted to slide off, he stopped her with a raised hand. "Stay. You don't weigh enough to make a difference."

"And it wouldn't hurt for a little distance, right?" she observed, still smarting from the moment.

"The only distance I'm worried about right now is between us and Trygg's hired guns. Whether they are Al Asheera or mercenaries," Booker replied. "How much do you know about desert survival?"

"Enough to know we're in serious trouble."

Chapter Eight

"Watch out!"

A wail of temper hit the air and jaws snapped at Booker's shoulder.

"Damn horse," he roared, then glanced at his shoulder, saw the small line of red marring the T-shirt.

"Are you okay?" Sandra patted the horse's neck from her seat in the saddle, felt the muscles quiver beneath her touch.

"Something's got him spooked."

Her eyes scanned the stretch of sand around them, glaring in the evening sun.

Booker grabbed the reins, held them tight in his hand. Then talked in low, easy whispers. The horse tugged once, then lowered his head with a snort.

"Now we have an understanding." Booker rubbed his nose, then loosened the reins. "Good boy."

"How are you with kids?" Sandra asked jokingly, but the soothing tone, the gentle movements, caught at her. She found herself wondering if he'd be a good father.

Booker swung up behind her. "Don't know any kids," he answered. "I understand horses because I spent most of my childhood on Texas ranches."

"You don't know—" Sandra's jaw tightened. "Quamar and Jarek's children?"

"I don't have the same kind of relationship with the royals that you do, Doc. I'm the hired help," he said, the stern edge back in his tone, the aloofness rigid in his muscles.

"You're more than that to them. I know for a fact Quamar and Jarek consider you a good friend."

"I imagine they are rethinking their position right about now."

"I'd be disappointed in them if they did," she answered softly.

Booker's gaze met Sandra's, and he tried not to read too much into the flash of truth.

"Tourlay is a day of travel from here by horse," he explained, directing the conversation back to their predicament. "We can get there by midnight. About an hour beyond Tourlay is the airstrip."

"Why the airstrip?"

"You're going back to the States," he answered. "After you give me your best guess at their location."

"And the cylinders? Where do you think they're going?"

"With me," he replied.

"Those cylinders are worthless without me," she managed through her anger.

"I don't care. Your life—"

"Is mine, alone," Sandra snapped, cutting him off. "And I've been living this nightmare for five years. Now I have the opportunity to correct what mistakes I can." She turned in the saddle. Her eyes narrowed. "And nothing, especially you, McKnight, will stop me."

"Is that right?"

"Yes." She gripped the pummel in fisted hands and resisted the impulse to punch the arrogance from his face. "That's right."

She turned to the front, her spine rigid, her eyes forward. "We're in this together or I do it alone, Booker. That's the deal. Take it or leave it."

Without warning, the horse cried out and reared back.

"Hold tight!" Booker yelled, but the order came too late. The horse jerked, breaking the reins free from Booker's grip. Sandra grappled to keep her seat.

Booker reached for her, but the animal shifted in one violent, sweeping movement.

Sandra screamed, grabbed for the horse and caught only air. She hit the ground hard, the breath punched from her lungs.

The horse came down, stamping the ground with his hooves.

Booker dived under the horse, hit the ground and rolled over Sandra, putting himself between her and the horse's hooves.

The horse stomped. The hoof hit the back of his head. Pain exploded through Booker's skull.

"Booker!" Sandra reached around, hugged his head with her arms, then struck at the horse with her heels.

The horse howled, then took off over the dunes, the reins dragging behind him.

"I should've shot the stupid—" Booker swore, blinked against the blurred vision. "Look around, Doc. Find what spooked him."

Sandra scanned the sand, saw the shift. A red tidal wave across the sand.

"Fire ants. Swarm," she gasped. "Too wide to dodge on foot."

Nausea swirled in Booker's stomach, slapped at the back of his throat. He staggered to his feet. The pain cleaved his skull; blood trickled down the back of his neck.

Sandra looked at his eyes, saw the lopsided dilation.

"Booker." She grabbed his chin, checked first one, then the other eye in the morning light, caught the haze of confusion in his gaze. "Hold on, damn it."

Quickly, she checked for other injuries. Blood

pooled at the back collar of his shirt; she probed the cut at his hairline with her fingers.

"If you lose blood, we could be in trouble," she murmured.

"You have no idea."

She stopped, frowned. "What do you mean?"

"I'm AB negative, Doc," Booker retorted. "Rare blood types can mess a guy up when he's out in the middle of nowhere."

"Damn it, Booker—"

"Leave it. We need to move," he snapped weakly. "I'll be fine. Been hurt worse."

He took a step, and his knees buckled. Sandra grabbed his arm to keep him upright. "Hold on."

"Fire ants have scouts," he warned. "We've got to put distance between them and us."

"I know. I was raised here, remember?" Once a scout ant attached itself to her or Booker, the others would swarm them. A swarm of fire ants had been known to envelop livestock, pick it clean and move on in mere minutes.

Booker grunted, but managed to move his feet through the sand. "Over the dune…rock formations. Higher ground. Give us time."

"No." She scanned the area for brush, trying to keep her head as the army of ants drew closer. "We fight fire ants with fire."

"Fire," he grunted, trying desperately to gain his

equilibrium. He reached into his front pocket and pulled out a lighter. "Use this and my knife. Cut the brush. Circle it around us."

She moved them closer to the rocks, sat him on the nearest one. Pulled the knife from his sheath. Quickly she hacked at the nearby brush, relieved when the branches broke dry and brittle.

"Be ready. Smoke can be seen for miles," Booker muttered.

"One enemy at a time." She placed the brush low in a ten-foot circle around them and struck the lighter.

The flames leaped to life, giving her a moment of safety. Booker shifted, then groaned. His face whitened.

"I need to examine your wound." She lifted her medical bag from her shoulder.

"We have more important problems right now. The damn horse took the supplies and water. Besides, I can see the concussion from this side," he snapped, but his words were badly slurred. He locked his legs under him to stand.

"Hold on, damn it." But she was too late. Booker's head lolled back and he slumped back onto the ground, unconscious.

"If you'd just given me a minute," Sandra muttered. Anger and frustration clashed, setting her jaw. "Arrogant superhero stereotype—"

Sandra stopped. Engines roared in the distance. She jumped the fire ring and scrambled up a nearby boulder.

Time had run out.

Two jeeps. Four men. Rifles. Just over the nearest dune.

Sandra jumped from the rock, made her way back to Booker. The sea of ants stood between them and the jeeps, giving Sandra some time.

Quickly, she plowed up the sand at the base with her hands. She rolled him into the shallow hole, tossed his pistol beside him and shoved the scrub over him, praying the smoke, brush and rock hid him.

Suddenly a flamethrower ignited; its flames spewed over the army of ants, burning them.

The acid scent of fuel and burned insects caught in her nose. "Handy," she muttered and palmed a nearby rock. "Why didn't we have one of those?"

Two of the men hopped from their vehicles, leaving the drivers of the jeeps to follow.

No use hiding. She wasn't armed and couldn't outrun a bullet. And she wouldn't leave Booker, until she was sure he'd be safe.

The first one, the shorter of the two, smiled at her. The sweaty features and huge lips filled with conceit.

"Where is the man, Doctor Haddad? McKnight?"

"He's dead."

The man hesitated, his eyes scanned the area briefly, touching on the boulder before moving back to her. "How?"

"Snakebite. Viper." Sand vipers were a well-known danger in the desert. Their venom lethal.

The second jeep stopped a few yards away.

A tall man approached, and the arrogance of his stride told Sandra he was the leader.

"Good work, Itamar."

Dressed in white with a red scarf wrapped around his head, he'd left one end loose against his shoulder, exposing his features. His right eye was covered by a black patch, but the other black iris burned with anticipation.

"She said McKnight is dead, Waseem. Viper bite."

"You've survived the desert on your own?" Waseem asked, disbelief in the glance he sent the other three men, the twitch of arrogance at the edge of his lips.

Her chin went up. "Yes."

"You don't mind then, if I make sure," he said, then turned to the two drivers. Both faces red from the sun. "Search the area and see if you can find his body. If he died, it hasn't been that long. Even dead he is worth money to us."

"We wait?" Itamar asked, frowning.

"No," Waseem replied, his eyes scanning the terrain. "We'll take her back to our camp and meet them there." The arrogance twisted into a tight, foreboding smile. "I have a few unanswered questions I wish to ask before we take her to Minos."

"Minos?" Sandra questioned, surprised.

"Go to the rocks," Waseem ordered the two men, ignoring Sandra. "Start there, then work your way out and around. If you don't find him, get in the jeep and make the circle wider until you do."

"You're wasting your time. He's buried miles from here."

"We'll see," the leader replied, his eyes on the drivers.

"Someone was here with her. If it was McKnight, he's gone," the first shouted from beside the boulder. "Whoever it is has left footprints. A male from the size of them."

"Search the area," Waseem yelled, then he turned to Sandra. "You lied."

She shrugged, relieved Booker got away. "Think what you want."

"What I think is that McKnight hides behind a woman. That he left you here to die when he saw us coming," Waseem answered. "I was told he was your protector."

"I need no one's help," she snapped, but she couldn't shake the thread of truth in the Al Asheera's words. "Especially from a dead man."

Waseem laughed, showing a row of white teeth.

"How long did you think you'd survive without any supplies?"

She nodded pointedly at the guns. "Your concern for my welfare touches me. But you needn't bother."

"Not you," he mused, his grin now vicious. "What you represent. Profit. General Trygg will pay handsomely for your safe return—do you not think so?"

"King Jarek will pay you more than General Trygg ever could."

"Is that so?" Waseem rubbed the side of his nose thoughtfully. "Trygg put out a bounty of a million for you. And for your friend."

Sandra laughed with derision. "How well do you know Trygg?"

"Well enough."

"I know him better. Which is why he wants me so bad," Sandra scoffed. "You're an idiot. Trygg will kill you before he'd actually pay you."

The punch came from nowhere. Stars exploded in her temple, the pain jagged and mean. Sandra fell to her knees.

"You assume much, Doctor," Waseem mused, his smile wicked. He shook out the sting in his hand.

A scream echoed off the dunes. An agonizing, almost inhuman scream that sent a chill up Sandra's spine, nerves dancing in her stomach.

"What is it?" Sandra asked, suddenly more afraid of the scream than of Waseem.

Itamar swore. "Our driver." He raised his rifle and surveyed the terrain through the scope.

Waseem grabbed Sandra, pulled her in front of him. The leader searched for cover, spotting the jeep several yards away.

Itamar shook his head. "We'll never make it. We're caught in the open."

Gunfire rang out, strafing the jeep radiators. Blowing them out. Making the vehicles useless.

"You have what is mine, Waseem. Let her go and I might let you live." Booker's voice boomed off the sands, the tone harsh, the words clipped.

"How did he know your name?" Itamar asked.

"The drivers, idiot." Waseem scanned the horizon, his eyes narrowing against the glare of the sun. "And if I don't?" he yelled.

A gunshot ricocheted, punctuating the leader's question.

Itamar grunted. He looked down at his chest where blood blossomed across the white of his shirt. He sank to his knees and hit the ground face-first.

Another scream hit the air. Followed by whimpering. "Your drivers have been very cooperative. Surprising what losing a finger one at a time will convince a man to do," Booker announced.

Waseem grabbed Sandra by her hair. She cried out in pain. He forced her down on her knees and crouched beside her, placing his knife at her neck.

"That's a mistake, Waseem," Booker yelled from behind the dune.

The whimpering grew louder from the darkness. "Now your friends here, the ones crying like a baby? They're already dead. But you can live if you let go of the doc. Immediately."

"If you don't come out now, McKnight, unarmed, Doctor Haddad will die before I do."

Steel bit into her neck, forcing Sandra to take shallow breaths. While his hand was steady, she felt his heart racing against his chest, his rapid breathing.

Fear?

Sandra decided to play into the possibility. Use it as a weapon. "He'll kill you if you hurt me. The last man who touched me died with a knife in the back of his head."

"I think he will do nothing while I have you." He tightened his grip until she cried out.

Sandra caught the whisper of movement. Heard Waseem grunt. Suddenly, the leader dropped her and his pistol. Blood poured from his arm, the wrist nearly severed.

Sandra stumbled away. She looked up, saw Booker holding a machete over the injured Al Asheera, who lay on his back, hugging his arm, moaning in agony.

Booker kicked the pistol toward Sandra. His features were pale, drawn. She saw him sway a bit on his feet, understood how unsteady he really was. It added to the dangerous set of his features, the edge of his temper.

"Get out of here, Sandra," he said, low and mean. "Take the pistol and walk up the path about a hundred yards. The horse returned. I tied him to the brush behind a cluster of boulders."

"Booker—" she answered, not knowing what was going to happen.

"You actually thought I'd leave you to them?" He glared at her. "Don't ever make yourself a target again."

"He's going to kill me, Doctor Haddad, then turn you in to Trygg himself," Waseem bit out.

"Your men mentioned Minos. The new Al Asheera leader. Then they died." Booker's features hardened. "I'm hoping for better information from you."

"And if I disappoint you?" the man sneered.

"The ants are feeding on your friends as we speak," Booker stated.

Waseem physically blanched.

"Booker—"

"Leave," he advised, his eyes flickering over Sandra. "Now."

From her estimate, he had very little time left on his feet, but sheer stubbornness was going to get him his answers.

She picked up the gun, not sparing Waseem a glance. There was no doubt in her mind that

Waseem had planned much worse for her. She could not stir any pity for him. "You have a half hour. Then I'm coming back."

"It won't take that long."

TIME PASSED AND BOOKER didn't show, so she grabbed the horse's reins.

When the gunshot sounded, all she could do was feel relief. Straight to the heart, as if he was putting a rabid dog out of its misery. Something she'd seen her Bari and the others do a million...

Then she heard it, the heavy shuffle of feet against the dirt.

Booker broke into the clearing, his face gray, his body sluggish. "Get on the horse, Doc," he ordered grimly. "Nothing left here."

She stopped herself from reaching for him. Knowing if she offered to help, the argument from him would make his head worse and drain more of his strength.

Once Sandra was on, Booker mounted up behind her. He leaned into her, more deadweight than not.

He took the reins, tugged, and the horse started toward the foothills.

"Can I ask you a question?"

"Is it worth three men's lives to save yours?" Booker snapped. "Yes."

She'd wrestled with her conscience during the time she waited. Those men were going to kill Booker.

"No," she said honestly. "You're hurt. We could've used one of those jeeps right about now."

"I wanted to make sure they weren't going anywhere with you," he acknowledged, then patted the horse's neck. "And Sam came back for me."

THE MALAQUO OASIS WAS little more than a water hole surrounded by indigenous plants and trees. It fed into wells across the foothills where villages lay.

Still, it provided plenty of shelter and water to help them recover. And privacy.

Booker's skull throbbed, but he hung on to his consciousness. He forced his eyes to focus on the area. "We'll stop here."

He slid off the horse, but his legs didn't support him. Pain shot through his hips as his knees slammed into the ground.

Darkness edged in on his vision. He fought it off.

"From the looks of you, we have little choice," Sandra said impatiently. "We should have stopped hours ago."

"We needed water and shade."

"What you need is rest, Booker," Sandra shot back. "And that's doctor's orders."

When he took a step, his legs gave way. Sandra was there, catching him under his arm just before he pitched forward.

"Hold on, big guy," she murmured.

He grabbed the back of her neck, the weakness in his fingers proof of his fading strength.

Slowly, he brought her face to his. His mouth found hers. A butterfly kiss that fluttered, then settled into a promise of something more, something deeper.

If he'd been rough, she would have resisted. But a whisper of a kiss? One that left a longing for a time she'd never forgotten. Where she lay in his arms, their bodies entwined...

Sandra pulled back, locked her knees. Forced her thoughts back to the present. "Don't, Booker."

Twenty-four hours of watching her being tied up, beat up, shot at, was enough for any reasonable man to question his sanity. Never before had he lost all control, never had he wanted to strangle and make love to a woman at the same time.

He'd definitely lost his mind.

She lifted her chin, just a bit, but couldn't hide the sheen of tears. He wasn't having it. Those hurt puppy eyes weren't going to touch his heart this time. Or any other time.

But when he looked in them, he saw more than hurt. For the first time, Booker saw real fear. She'd faced the guns, the fire ants, a kidnapping, and not once did she show fear, except when she thought he would be killed.

"I needed to put a stop to your bossiness," he muttered. "It worked, didn't it?"

It worked. But that wasn't his typical "stop arguing" kiss. That was...

What?

Loving, he admitted.

"You're very lucky, McKnight. You're in no condition to rationalize," she warned, but the words were soft. "Otherwise, you'd be very afraid of me right now."

"Your anger doesn't scare me, Doc," Booker admitted, still tasting her on his mouth. "Not as much as..."

"As what?"

"Your stupid heroic ideas," Booker bit out, his frustration getting the best of him.

"Stupid—"

"You buried me...alive."

"You were unconscious!"

"Why didn't you use some of that ammonia in your medical bag to wake me up?"

"From a concussion? Seriously?" She shook her head. "I carry the ammonia to confuse any tracking dogs—" She froze midstep, her brows raised. "How did you know the contents of my bag?"

"I searched the bag while you were asleep on the horse," he muttered.

She took a few more steps, her movements stiff, jerking with anger.

"Not so rough, Doc." Jackhammers thrashed the

inside of his skull. "I don't have my legs under me yet."

"If I wasn't a *doctor,* I'd drop you on your head," she replied, her words sharp, but her arms instantly gentled around him.

"As long as I'm sitting down first."

"Fine," she agreed. "You had no right to search my things."

"I had every right," Booker corrected. "I'm trying to keep you alive, damn it. If you had the cylinders, we wouldn't even be having this discussion and I certainly wouldn't be dealing with the damn headache."

"Sit here." She settled Booker in a small clearing near the lagoon. Relief replaced her anger. At least he hadn't found anything in the bag.

"Take care of Sam, will you?" Booker lay back and shut his eyes against the sun. "Just lead him to the water—he'll do the rest."

"Why did you name him Sam?"

"After someone I once knew," he drawled, "who didn't come back for me."

Chapter Nine

Quamar stormed into the palace's main office. "You cannot do this, Jarek. You cannot issue an order for your guards and secret service to join in the search for Sandra."

"You forget I am king. I do what is necessary," Jarek snapped. "Sandra has been missing for over twenty-four hours. I want her found. She hasn't left the country through the checkpoints or airports. It means she's still out there."

"We do not have the manpower to protect the palace and to search the desert," Quamar reasoned. "She is with Booker."

"With our wives and children sent to the States for protection, we need no one else."

"Your duties—"

"Have been canceled, damn it!" Jarek said, his patience gone.

"Uncle Bari has offered the men from his caravan," Quamar offered.

Bari Al Asadi, even after abdicating, still had

many men who stayed with his nomad ways, following his caravan. Men who fought against the Al Asheera years before.

"They were once soldiers…most are too old now. They are no longer able to fight off trained mercenaries."

"He has a hundred men—"

"We need ten times that many, Quamar," Jarek replied slowly. "I convinced Cain to send some American troops here to help."

"And?"

"Someone on Capitol Hill blocked his order. Cain flew back this morning to find out who."

Quamar knew Cain well enough that heads would be rolling once he hit the States. "Is President Mercer aware of this?"

"No. Cain suspects whoever blocked the order might be the same person who helped Trygg escape. And might deal directly with the Oval Office."

"When Mercer finds out Cain is keeping him in the dark—and he will—Cain will be flayed alive." A strategist, Cain's reasoning was always sound. But President Mercer had an Irish temper that never fit in any equation.

The intercom clicked on. "Your Majesty."

Jarek hit the button. "Yes, Trizal."

"Dr. and Mrs. Omar Haddad are here to see you."

Jarek glanced up at Quamar. "Do you want to explain our problems with manpower to them?"

Quamar sighed. "No, I do not."

With a curt nod, Jarek hit the button again. "Send them in."

"Yes, Your Majesty."

Omar Haddad wasn't a tall man, but he was fit for his age, with dark eyes and silver-gray hair that covered most of his head. Dark skin, with deep lines marring his features—more from worry, Quamar imagined, than the Sahara sun.

"Your Majesty." Omar's tone cut with censorship. "We are sorry to disturb you, but we couldn't wait around our quarters any longer without hearing a word from you."

Jarek acknowledged Omar's frustration with a nod, but it would not change his position on the matter. As a precaution, Jarek had ordered the Haddads to the palace and placed them under guard. He did not want Trygg using them as a weapon against Sandra.

"Have you found out anything, Your Majesty?"

"Not yet." Jarek took Elizabeth's hand in his and frowned at the icy feel of her skin. He covered it with his other hand to add his warmth. "Elizabeth, if there was news I would have sent it over at once."

"You haven't heard from Booker McKnight, then, either?" Omar asked, his eyes narrowed. It was apparent to Jarek that Omar did not trust Booker to take care of his daughter.

"No—"

"Are you looking?"

"The Sahara is thousands of square miles. It takes time—"

"I know this," Omar said. "This is my daughter we are talking about, Jarek."

He used his king's first name, a sign of family—one that Omar didn't often use to take advantage. Jarek sensed the extent of his friend's worry. He let the familiarity pass.

"I understand—"

"With all forgiveness, I do not believe you do, Your Majesty," Elizabeth said quietly, then looked to each man. English born, Elizabeth Haddad was steeped in blue-blooded culture. The daughter of a surgeon, she made the perfect wife for Omar. Trim, petite, with impeccable taste, she'd endured much over the years that tested her spine of steel.

"You both are husbands and you both have children. If your child disappeared, would you not worry? Would you not demand answers?" Elizabeth paused, the paleness of her skin evidence of the strain, the fear. "Would you not do everything in your means to bring her back, and those who have done her harm, to justice? If not for yourself, then for your wives?"

"What do you mean, 'everything in your means'?" Jarek questioned, purposefully looking beyond the despair to the couple's determination. Something was amiss, something that he could not put his finger on.

"I hope you have not done anything foolish, Omar," he said, then turned to the older woman. "Elizabeth?"

"What they are not telling you, Jarek, it that there is a bounty on Sandra's and Booker's heads." Sheik Bari Al Asadi entered the office unannounced—a privilege given only to the man who had abdicated his throne years before to Jarek's father, Makrad. "Omar has offered double the amount for the return of Sandra."

"How much is that, Father?" Quamar asked.

Hard-bitten and weathered, with a white beard and black eyes, Quamar understood his father, Bari, had little patience when those he loved were in danger. And while Sandra wasn't blood, Sheik Bari considered her a niece, and Omar his brother.

"Two million," Omar stated, his tone arrogant, almost defiant.

"Do you have two million?"

"I have means of getting it."

"And you know this how?" Jarek's tone matched his uncle's impatience.

"Mind your tongue, nephew." Bari's black eyes hardened, his tone sharpened by an innate royal edge. "Just because I am no longer king does not mean I no longer have loyal subjects. Or deserve the respect of my position."

"My apologies, Uncle." Jarek's jaw flexed, his impatience schooled behind set features. But he didn't back down. His uncle might once have been king, but Jarek still was. "At the end of the day, it is I who am responsible. Not you."

Bari gave a brief nod, accepting the explanation. "Trygg now has the Al Asheera hunting Booker and Sandra."

"The Al Asheera are no longer a threat," Jarek replied.

"I have heard whispers they have a new leader by the name of Minos."

Jarek waved his hand. "We obliterated their armies years ago. Those who survived are scattered over the desert."

"Even if only one is alive, they are still a threat, nephew. Do not ever forget it."

Chapter Ten

Sandra raised Booker's eyelid, checked the dilation with her flashlight and noted the one pupil was still not normal.

Earlier, she'd cleaned the wound, stitched it, then bandaged it to keep it protected.

He'd have a scar, but a small one compared to the others that tattooed his body. Several from knives, a few from bullets. One across his right knee from falling down a treacherous mountain.

It was part of his history, a part that he never shared with her.

The sky dimmed to a murky orange, losing its heat, allowing the shadows to grow, the night to settle in.

Sandra tossed more wood on the fire, risking discovery for the warmth, then led the horse to the water and grass.

Surviving the night was the most important thing right now. Many fires littered the desert.

Camps were everywhere, filled with nomads, tourists and caravans.

Fatigue made her legs shake. Sandra sat near Booker, taking a minute to gather some energy.

They'd lose a day here. A necessary delay. She wouldn't take chances with Booker's physical condition.

She wouldn't have another death on her conscience.

The strap of her medical bag caught at her neck. Sandra slipped it over her shoulders.

Of its own accord, her hand drifted over the thick seam in the back. It wouldn't be long before she'd need the map hidden in the lining.

Booker shifted, muttering in his sleep.

Her hand slipped over his forehead, then behind his neck. The heat of his skin nearly singed her fingers.

She silently cursed, knowing the concussion had brought on the fever.

She grabbed a bottle of water and the bottle of aspirin from her bag. It was all she had; she hoped it would be enough.

She slipped the aspirin toward the back of his tongue, then lifted his head. "Booker, wake up."

She shook him gently. Booker's eyes fluttered open. Fever and firelight turned the blue irises molten silver.

"Drink," she whispered. "Please."

"You're safe?" His voice shook, from fever or relief; it still troubled her. "I thought you died—"

"We're both safe for now, Booker," she assured him. "Drink some more water. You need to stay hydrated."

"We?" His eyes bored into hers. "You said *we*."

"Yes. We—"

"You and the baby. You're both okay?"

Sandra froze. "The baby?"

Booker glared at her, his eyes hazy from distant memories. "The baby, Emily. Remember? Our baby?"

"Booker, it's Sandra. Not Emily." She placed the bottle at his lips, coaxed him to take a few sips. Shivers rippled over his skin, caused his shoulders to shake.

"Damn cold," Booker muttered. "Where's the jungle? Why Siberia?"

"We're in the desert," Sandra soothed. The temperature was dropping quickly out here. The fire wouldn't be enough. Not with a fever raging.

"You'll be warm soon. I promise." She lowered his head, then took off her shoes, stripped down to her T-shirt and panties. She burrowed beside him, rubbing herself against the coldness of his skin, cradled his head against her shoulder and closed her eyes.

But his words whispered through her mind.

The baby, Emily. Our baby.

"Sandra?" Booker rasped out, the desperation in his tone ragged. He pulled her across his chest, cupped her chin in his hand.

"Yes?" she answered, wanting what he offered, knowing he did so in his dreams. "You've got a fever, Booker. You need rest."

His arms tightened when she shifted, pinning her to the length of his body. His eyes filmed over with a blue haze, raced over her face. "God, you're beautiful."

Then his mouth covered hers. Hot, feverish, it demanded, no begged, a response.

"Booker, please." Now she was the one who begged.

On a groan, he deepened the kiss and her will broke.

Tongue swept against tongue, rubbing, seducing in soft, sensual circles. Then his mouth moved to her lower lip, drawing it between his own, nipping and suckling until her toes curled, her limbs shook, her body thrust against his in a desperate attempt to end the torture, or continue it, she couldn't be sure. Didn't care.

Her hands found his shoulders, drew him down on her. His skin slid against hers, hot and feverish. His body trembled, then shivered, then shuddered.

Sandra crashed into reality. Felt him shudder again. Fever induced, not desire driven.

"Booker. You're not well." She grabbed his shoulder, pushed him away, let him roll to her side. "You need rest."

He groaned once, then didn't stir.

Chapter Eleven

Pain drove Booker awake, but panic and fear opened his eyes. Startled, he reached for his gun. The pain—sharp and white-hot—speared his shoulder, tore through his neck.

He remembered then. The horse's hooves. The fight with the mercenaries.

Waseem's admission before he died.

The new leader of the Al Asheera, a man named Minos, wanted Sandra. Wanted whatever she was hiding from Trygg.

He saw her then, waist deep in the water. Her gun left on a rock, less than a foot from her elbow.

Smart woman.

He leaned back, angry at the relief that weakened his limbs. Made his heart beat hard.

She'd left her clothes by the rocks to dry. She wore only her bra and, he assumed, her underpants.

Slowly, she turned her back to him.

He hissed through his teeth.

Bruises tattooed her body. Brown and blue. Dark and ugly.

She stepped from the water. The sunlight hit her dark hair, caught the lighter strands, the auburn highlights, set them on fire. Small, supple curves were wrapped up in flesh-colored panties, topped with a small bow at the top of the elastic.

Desire tightened his gut, fisted his hands with frustration.

Jaw clenched, he battled through the pain, forced down the desire.

But he couldn't force himself to close his eyes.

Sandra stopped midstride when she saw him, then her features instantly became unreadable as she shuttered her thoughts from him. Slowly she emerged from the water.

"You're awake." She stopped long enough to grab the pistol, clothes and, he noted, her medical bag before she joined him.

Like he said before, smart woman.

He started to nod, then decided against it when the pain morphed into a concert of jackhammers inside his skull.

"Just." He shifted from underneath the lean-to she'd built, then glanced up at the sky, noted the direction of the sun above them, felt the prick of late-afternoon heat on his skin.

"I saw your bruises."

Quickly she slipped into her semidry T-shirt and pants. "They look worse than they feel."

It took effort, but he stood, his legs shaking in protest. He cupped her cheek, ran a soft thumb over her jaw where the shadow of a bruise remained. "You gave better than you got, Doc."

The gentleness of his compliment nearly undid her after the worry she lived through the night before. Slowly, she turned her cheek away, watched his hand drop to his side, curl back into a fist.

"You had a fever most of the night," Sandra said, her voice even. She opened her medical bag and grabbed two pills. "Here, take these." She handed him the pills and the water. "It will take the edge off the pain and ease the soreness. You'll get your strength back quicker."

"Time is short, Doc." Booker downed the medicine. "We need to get going. We can make Tourlay just after sunset."

"A day of rest is more important—"

"Waseem told me that the Al Asheera are rising again. They have a leader. Minos. I can't be sure whether Jarek knows about him. If this new leader has infiltrated Jarek's people, I want to make sure you're out of harm's way before the war starts."

"I know of Minos, Booker. He is a peaceful leader. He cares for his people."

"They aren't working for Trygg. He's a tool for them to get close to you. One of the men in Trygg's camp has ties to the Al Asheera. He's been feeding Intel back to Minos."

"The Al Asheera would not risk a relationship with Trygg. It would put them in direct opposition to the crown," she argued. Sandra had gotten to know these people. Some she even called friends. They would never follow a man like Trygg.

"They want the cylinders," Booker stated with derision. "They will destroy their enemies with one or two of the cylinders, then sell the rest to the highest bidder. The money will come in handy when they seize Taer."

"Destroy their enemies? You mean the royals?"

"One tidy little package," Booker scoffed. "Waseem had knowledge of your new weapon going on the black market. He didn't know what that weapon was exactly."

"He could've been lying to you."

"He wasn't lying," Booker responded flatly. Waseem spent the last fifteen minutes of his life begging to stay alive. He would have betrayed his own mother to save his skin.

"Minos and his followers have joined the game," he said, not masking the truth this time. "Like I said, they might not know what you have, Doc, but they know you have something. And they know it's a weapon."

"The Al Asheera are no longer vengeful." A sadness stretched across her chest, a heavy band that tightened with each breath. "Waseem and some others must have broken away from the main tribe."

"They are all dangerous, until proven otherwise," Booker commented casually, but those blue eyes were anything but as they swept over her pale features. "One, two, a half-dozen bad ones—any more than one just becomes a number."

"I can prove the Al Asheera are not in league with Trygg," she stated, steel now in her tone, her feet back under her. She took a step to him, then another, until they were almost toe to toe.

"It's time for you to trust me." Her chin lifted higher until her gaze locked with his. "I have connections in Tourlay. Connections that are not influenced by Trygg. We can stay here for twenty-four hours, then we'll find my friends. They'll help us get to the cylinders quicker."

"That is not going to happen."

"Give me one good reason why not?"

"Let's start with your capabilities," Booker stated. "The reason I'm in this condition? Saving you. The reason it got worse? Saving you again. And that doesn't even include the apartment the other night, when I saved you the first time."

"I didn't ask—"

"My turn," he interrupted, the two words cutting through the air like the crack of a whip. "Now, back in the day of *your* ancestors, I'd own you."

"That's ridiculous—"

"Still talking," Booker warned.

Sandra placed her hands on her hips, not happy.

"Now," Booker continued, "because I respect your medical abilities—to a point—we'll take a few hours, until the heat lessens, then we'll move."

"You need rest," Sandra replied, her voice hard with a doctor's impatience. "Why on earth would you risk serious complications—"

"Because frankly, I'm not up to the task of saving you a fourth time. And staying here too long will make us easy targets. Is that clear?"

She couldn't argue with that, as much as she wanted to.

But it was the fatigue that overtook his features— just for a second. Just long enough to remind her that he was suffering.

"Do I have a choice?"

"Yes. You can tell me where the cylinders are, and stay put somewhere safe."

"No. We're in this together."

"Noted," he said grimly. He eased back against the rock, dismissing her. "Now if we're done—"

Frustration bubbled, until it spit angry sparks that sizzled and snapped at her nerves. "Not quite. You still need to tell me about Emily. And your baby."

Chapter Twelve

Night covered the city of Tourlay. The streetlamps burned a dull, misty yellow, thickening the smoke spewing from the roof holes of nearby dwellings. Buildings that had years before lost their charm— their bricks now gouged, the paint long replaced with graffiti.

"Follow me." Booker kept to the shadows, peering in windows they passed.

"Are you looking for a place?" Sandra asked, making sure she kept within a few steps. "Because I know of one up the street."

His eyes studied her face for a moment, but he didn't ask how she knew. "Okay. Show me."

The dwelling was little more than a room with a roof, gutted long before by its original owners, or nomads like Booker and Sandra who sought shelter. Dirt floors, clay walls and a roof made of scrap lumber, it did little more than protect them from the elements.

Sandra stepped through the door after Booker

gave her the "all clear." "The family that lived here, they had moved on to better things."

"You helped them?"

"Not as much as I wanted to."

Booker nodded. "Stay here. Keep away from the windows and door. I'll be back in a while." Before she could respond, he stepped out into the darkness.

In the back corner, near the only window, lay a small circle of stone for fire.

With the dry wood for the roof, Sandra decided against tempting fate and hugged her arms to her chest.

She was my wife, long before I met you. She died from complications when our baby miscarried.

Also long before I met you.

And frankly, its none of your damn business, Doc.

That was it. That's all he'd said.

And he was right.

It wasn't any of her business.

But the hurt was there, a razor-sharp edge that sliced the air between them.

The door creaked. Before she could react, he stood in front of her.

"Take this." Booker handed her a bundle. Harsh woven cloth scraped against her palm.

"A change of clothes," he whispered. "Put it on."

"Where—"

"A caftan from a nearby laundry line."

It took a moment, but she found the openings, slipped the garment over her head.

"So we can move through the streets easier." He pulled a duplicate over his head.

Both were dark and blended well with the night. She took a step, testing the length, pleased when the hem brushed against the top of her foot. If she had to run, she didn't want to trip.

Sandra drew a shabby scarf from the bottom of the bag, and noticed the flat bread and cheese. "You've been busy."

"I also found a place to stable the horse." A pail clattered somewhere down the street. People shouted; a door slammed. Booker placed a finger to his lips, then peered out the window for a long moment.

Two men, their backs hunched, hurried down a nearby alleyway. Obviously, they didn't like the noise or the skirmish it caused.

Sandra draped the scarf around her neck, then pulled out the food, divided it in half and put the first portion back in the bag.

When he stepped from the window, she held out his share. A small piece of bread and cheese. "Digestion dehydrates. It's best to have small meals."

Booker waved off the food. "I'm not hungry."

"Doesn't matter. You need to eat something." She lifted her hand higher. "I won't be able to carry you if you faint. So I'll leave you where you fall and finish this…hunt…by myself."

"Hunt?" he questioned, but took the bread and cheese.

"I'm sorry, should I have said 'vacation'?"

Booker took a bite of the cheese. His head pounded, tiny razor-sharp claws raking it from the inside every time his jaw moved.

"The cylinders are in the mountains on the farthest side of Tourlay. Easily a full day by jeep from the city."

"We're going to need supplies."

"My friends will provide them."

"Just how friendly are we talking here?" He took another bite, this time out of sheer stubbornness. The pain ebbed quicker, but not quick enough. He stepped over to the window, took another long look.

"I know more people than you think," Sandra argued. "Last year, I found the contacts, got introduced to the right people on the streets who could provide the services I required or the supplies I needed in cities throughout Taer."

"What do you mean? Right people?" Anger whipped his head around, but the dizziness had him locking his knees, grabbing the window's edge with his free hand.

"You need rest, Booker."

"I need a hell of a lot more than that," he quipped. "Finish telling me about your contacts all over Taer."

"Tourlay had been one of the main cities I worked in. I've spent the last year relocating families, providing medical treatment."

Booker swore silently. "Who helped you?"

"I can't tell you."

Guilt edged her eyes, but defiance lifted her chin. Obviously, it was her choice of penance.

A dangerous one.

"They're wanted by Taer. They're Al Asheera, Booker."

"Who are they, Doc?" His voice was silky smooth and razor-sharp.

"I can't tell you…I have to show you. They'll only deal with me. It took me months to arrange my first meeting with them." She folded her arms for emphasis.

"All right." He held out his hand, helped her to her feet. "Let's go."

She glanced at his hand, remembered the strength of his fingers against her skin….

She tugged free, wiped her palms against her pant legs. His words replayed in her head.

Suspicious, she studied him, searching for the hidden agenda. "You gave in too easy, McKnight. What's the catch?"

"No catch. It's logical. We don't have the time for me to find someone through back channels. We'd lose several days. And we need supplies. Weapons.

Climbing gear. We have no idea what condition the trails are in."

"So you're agreeing with me?"

"Looks like I am." Booker scowled. "Don't get used to it, Doc."

"Oh, I won't." She didn't stop the smile.

They slipped into a back alley down the street. "Go ahead of me," he ordered softly.

"Why?"

"Just do it," Booker snapped, his voice low. "I want to make sure we're not being followed."

She glanced around, alert. "Fine," she muttered. "I always wanted to be human bait."

"Not bait. Just a distraction." Booker scanned the perimeter, keeping a few steps behind Sandra. "And I've got your back. So don't worry."

"Should I whistle a happy tune?"

When he didn't answer, she sighed and started down the street.

Booker counted to ten, then stepped from the shadows.

Suddenly, two men emerged from the alley. They crossed the street, their faces covered by scarves.

Booker kept out of the streetlights, followed along the edge of the buildings.

Sandra stepped into the lamplight, her steps stiff. It took all her willpower, but she didn't glance over her shoulder.

Brave woman, Booker acknowledged. The men

ate up the ground behind her, making their presence felt on the quiet street.

Sandra kept her pace steady, her head straight ahead.

Booker ducked down a nearby alley, one he'd traversed earlier. He jogged to the end, up another street and down another back street. He came out a few feet in front of Sandra. When she stepped past, he grabbed her arm.

She didn't scream, but she threw a punch. He caught her fist in his, locked her arms behind her.

Her heel came down on his instep.

"Damn it, Doc!" His breath hissed between his teeth as the pain shot up his leg.

Her heart raced against his chest. "It's me." He shook her to break through the panic and fear.

"Booker?" She swore, her fear now anger. He let her go and stepped back.

Her hand free, she swung, connected with his temple. "You son of a—"

"Stop it." He gripped her wrist, ignored the jab of pain that pierced his skull, the razor-sharp stars that imploded in his head. "You hit me in the head, with a concussion."

"I'll fix it later." She yanked her hand free. "Next time whistle or something before you sneak up on me again."

"I'll remember." He jabbed a finger in the general

direction behind him. "Go down the alley, and hide in the doorway on the left. Be quiet."

The annoyance morphed into anger. "That works well for you, doesn't it? Telling people what to do."

"Only when they actually do what they're told." He eased up to the corner, took a look up the street. "So go. Now."

The men glanced around, searching for their target, their semiautomatic pistols out, ready.

No talking, their footsteps light. Their hands up, signaling.

Military hand singles.

Not the Al Asheera.

Trygg's mercenaries.

Booker waited until both breached the alleyway, then he stepped from the shadows. "Looking for me, gentlemen?"

The first man swung his pistol toward Booker, but he was too late. Booker shifted, turned and twisted the man's arm. He heard a snap of bone, the cry of pain. He rammed his elbow into the man's throat, yanked the pistol free and let him fall to the ground.

Booker swung around with a high kick. His foot connected with the other mercenary's wrist. Again a snap, but this one took the pain with a grunt, then threw a fist.

Booker's jaw slammed shut, his head snapped

back. He staggered under the explosion of pain that rocked his head, rattled his teeth.

"That all you got, McKnight?"

"No. He's got me," Sandra retorted. The man swung around. Sandra kicked him in the crotch.

The man gasped, went down on his knees, then hit the ground, rolling in agony.

Booker picked up the discarded pistols, spared the injured men a glance, his mouth grim.

"I definitely will whistle next time, Doc." Light-headed, Booker locked his knees. Bile slapped at the back of his throat.

"Glock. Semiautomatics. Matching set. Same as your friends we ran into yesterday." He hit the release, checked the clip. "Full. Ready for battle." He tucked one pistol in his belt, handed the other to Sandra. "Put this away in case you need it later."

"Really?" She took the gun, slipped it into the bag. "That must have been a hard decision."

"It would be harder to watch you hurt," Booker admitted, annoyed.

Startled, Sandra glanced at him. "Booker—"

"I ordered you to stay in the doorway."

"It was an order?" she quipped, not quite catching the light tone. "I thought it was a suggestion."

The second man struggled to get up. Booker kicked him in the head, knocking him unconscious. At least now someone else's headache would be worse than his. "Time to go."

THE WAREHOUSE STOOD AT the edge of the desert, nudging the main rail yard and its web of tracks.

"You need to stay out here." Sandra spoke in hushed tones. The building stood twenty feet tall, its walls spider-cracked cement, its compound fenced and deserted.

And pitch-black.

"I don't want to spook them." She lifted the latch on a small gate cut in the fencing, cringed when it squeaked in protest.

"The hell I am," he growled. He pulled the Glock free from his waistband, thumbed off the safety.

She slapped a hand on his chest, pushed enough to get his attention. "Listen to me. I can do this."

The blue eyes darkened, and his heartbeat strengthened beneath her palm. Its tempo slow, steady. She curled her fingers, just a bit, until the warmth of his skin penetrated the thin cotton of his clothes, seeped into her palm until her nerves jumped.

"You have no idea what you're asking." His hand moved over hers, stroking the wrist with his thumb. Her pulse jumped, her own heart raced.

Her eyes snapped to his, not sure they were still talking about the warehouse. "I'm asking you to trust me. Give me five minutes by myself."

"And if I think the situation is getting out of control, you'll do what I ask?" His thumb continued to stroke her wrist, muddling her thoughts. She tugged her hand free. Resisted the urge to shake the tingling away.

"Yes," she agreed, realizing he'd make them stand there all night out of stubbornness. "But if I'm right and arrange everything we need, you'll let me make more of the decisions. Deal?"

"Let's get through this first." He glanced at his watch. "Five minutes, Doc."

"It's all I'm going to need." In a quick trot, she crossed the yard and slipped through the warehouse door.

Booker counted a slow ten, then followed her in.

Stacks of wood crates surrounded him. Some topping fifteen feet. Some shorter. Some left solitary by the nearest wall.

Most smelled of gas and fresh wood. And something else. Booker inhaled. Gun grease.

He pried the top off a nearby crate with his knife. AK-47s.

He moved to another. Pried the top free.

Rocket launchers. Land mines.

Booker swore. What the hell was Sandra thinking by getting in the middle of this?

Quickly, he searched the shipment, found explosive disks similar to those he used against the helicopter. He grabbed the nearest one, noting its slightly larger size, the advanced detonation device.

American made, he thought grimly.

He punched in a time span on its small digital

keypad, then shoved it between two of the crates filled with the land mines.

With light steps, he made his way to the office. A giant with no neck and a hairy face stood by the door. An M16 short-stocked machine gun crooked in his arm.

Sandra's scream ricocheted through the walls.

The giant's teeth, broken and yellow, split into a big grin. Booker peered through the narrow window at the top of the office door.

"Hey, ugly."

Startled, the big guy swung around, his machine gun leveled. Booker stepped in, grabbed the gun and shoved the barrel under the giant's chin.

His finger pinned the guard's against the trigger. Slowly, he applied pressure.

The giant's eyes widened.

"You can move your hands off the gun, or eat a bullet. Your choice."

Slowly, the man dropped the weapon and raised his hands above his shoulders.

"We're going through that door," Booker warned, leaving no doubt that the giant would be his human shield. He patted the man down, tossed away the knife hidden at his ankle, then took the set of car keys from the giant's pocket and shoved them into his own.

"Let's go." Booker waved the gun toward the door. "Quietly."

The guard nodded, then opened the door.

Two men stood across the room. Both holding M16s. Both pointed at Sandra.

"Friends of yours?" Booker asked Sandra, his eyes on the two men.

"Don't you dare say it," she snapped, her features flushed pink with either humiliation or rage, he didn't know which.

"That I was right?"

"Don't push me, Booker." Her black eyes burned.

Definitely rage, Booker mused.

"If I may interrupt?" The oldest of the two stepped forward. He was a squat man, at least two feet shorter than his companion, with a round belly that strained the buttons of his sweat-soiled khaki shirt. His hair, peppered gray, hung long and thin just past his ears and framed a ruddy, square face with a fairly large nose and bug eyes.

Booker glanced from the older man to the younger. Noted the same nose and eyes.

Relatives. Always a touchy situation.

Since Ugly wasn't blood, Booker knew his bargaining chip just lost its value.

Booker slammed the weapon handle against the back of the giant's head. The man slid to the floor unconscious.

"Booker, meet the Contee brothers," Sandra said, her tone derisive. She jabbed a thumb toward the older, shorter brother. "This is Madu. The other is Boba. It seems they both are aware of the contract on our heads."

"And your friend?" Booker nudged Ugly with his foot.

Sandra shrugged. "Never met him before."

"Yemesi. Our boss felt the need for us to have added protection," Madu admitted with a shrug.

"Your boss needs to have another look at his staffing list," Booker remarked. "This man barely understands how to hold a gun."

"I agree. So you understand why we don't care if you killed him," Madu replied, his lips twisting into a slight sneer.

The office offered little space to maneuver. A steel desk was stamped with the U.S. Army logo, its top buried under piles of take-out cartons and papers. Behind it stood matching swivel office chairs on rollers and a single column of filing cabinets.

Booker's gaze shifted over the room, touched briefly on the chair behind Madu before he spotted the red scarf.

Booker dropped the pistol onto the floor near his feet. "The doc says there is good Al Asheera. I take it you're not one of them?"

"Our boss said you were smart. That we needed to be extra careful with you," Boba observed with a frown. Taller than Madu by six inches or more, the younger brother sported less of a belly and a more expensive hairstyle—slick against his scalp. But not enough to cover the receding hairline.

"Shut up, Boba! You talk too much." With a quick warning glance to his brother, Madu moved to the desk and settled himself into its chair.

Boba frowned. "Bloody hell, it doesn't matter anymore. We've got them, don't we?"

"You do." Booker held up his hands. "I give up. Before you kill me though, I'd like to at least know who ordered my death."

Sandra inhaled, reminding herself Booker had probably dealt with this situation a million times.

"I don't think you're so smart, McKnight." Madu raised his gun slightly, until the barrel pointed at Booker's forehead. He leaned back on his chair and placed his feet on the small clean corner of his desk. "Our orders are to bring you back with us. Not to kill you. We just didn't expect you to make our job so easy by walking through our front door."

"You're lying," Booker said quietly. "You knew Doctor Haddad would need supplies, and that you'd be one of the people she'd turn to, considering you've helped her in the past."

"The doctor, yes. Not you," Madu admitted. "When the boss said you wouldn't be far behind, I didn't believe him."

Sandra shook her head. "I don't understand."

"The reason you finally made contact with Madu last year, Doc, is because someone realized that the time would come that you'd need to trust the Contee brothers. This setup has been in the works for a year now."

"But all those families we helped—"

"We were ordered to help you." Madu snorted. "Of course, it's a bonus when it helps our people, too."

"Let me guess who your boss is," Booker stated flatly. "Minos?"

"Exactly," Madu admitted. "He hasn't been around long, but he has single-handedly brought possibility and pride back to our people. We will take back what is rightfully ours. With your help, of course."

"Maybe you aren't so smart, McKnight. You're on the wrong side." Boba smiled, revealing two gold incisors.

"I really thought you were decent men." Anger shook Sandra's voice.

"Don't be so hard on yourself, Doctor Haddad. We like you. You've done many good things for our people," Boba admitted. "This isn't personal. It's business. Isn't that right, Madu?"

"That's right," the older brother agreed and cocked the revolver. "Now it's time to take care of some other business, McKnight."

"We weren't supposed to kill him, Madu."

"A million dollars will help a lot of our people, Boba," Madu rationalized. "We'll tell the boss you got caught in a crossfire trying to be a hero. You understand."

"Actually, Madu, I don't think I do," Booker drawled, then glanced at Sandra. His eyes flashed with warning. "Down!"

Sandra dropped to the ground. The explosion pounded the air, sucking it dry of oxygen, clogged it with heat and smoke.

The air buzzed around her head, muffled her ears.

Booker rolled, grabbed his gun. Both Madu and his brother staggered to their feet. Madu groaned and doubled over.

Booker grabbed Sandra's arm. "Go!"

He pulled her out into the street and into a nearby alley. "What do we do now?" Sandra bent over, dragged oxygen into her lungs.

Booker held up a set of car keys, gave them a shake. "Where did you get those?"

"From Madu's guard. Yemesi." Booker clicked the button. Heard the beep of an alarm, saw the flash of headlights on a nearby silver-colored jeep.

"I think we just found our ride."

SENATOR KEITH HARPER TUGGED at his suit for the hundredth time. It was the middle of the night. The fact that he didn't have to battle the heat was little consolation.

Impatient, he reminded himself that this deal wouldn't be made unless he traveled over to this forsaken land.

He was a big man, more than six four, barrel-chested and broad shouldered. The muscle beneath was more solid than slackened from age.

At sixty-five, his face was creased from years of stress and politics, not from the harsh elements of field operations.

He'd come from ten generations of military strategists and diplomats, spent a few decades as a career officer, but many more as a senator on Capitol Hill, dealing with bureaucrats and their self-righteous rhetoric, buying their wives a nice dinner, their mistresses' even nicer jewelry.

The tent door rustled. A moment later, a man stepped in. He wore dark riding pants, a matching shirt and black leather boots. A scarf, bloodred, covered all but his granite-black eyes.

"General. I'm sorry for the delay," the man called Minos said, with no apology in the slow, drawn-out words.

He carried a whip, touched it to his forehead in a friendly salute. "You understand that most in our position have very little time between business dealings."

Instead of approaching the general, he crossed to a table set at the far end of the tent.

"Two hours is more than a little late, Minos."

"It could not be helped. One of my warehouses just went up in flames. I had to deal with the damage control. I lost thousands of American dollars' worth of merchandise," the Al Asheera leader stated unequivocally, then dropped the whip on the table. He grabbed the whiskey bottle, unscrewed the top and poured himself two fingers high. "Would you care for a drink?"

"No," Harper replied, his tone sharp, his impatience clear. He lifted the briefcase up slightly. "You've wasted too much of my time already. I have a flight to the States later tonight. And I don't want to be spotted here. Not when we are so close to our goal."

"You don't need to be concerned. The Sahara is vast, General. The twin-engine planes traveling to and from my camp are never noticed. I make sure of it. It's bad for business." Minos set the bottle down, raised his glass in a silent toast, then downed the whiskey under the scarf in one gulp.

"No one knows you are here." The black eyes narrowed, opaque and cool. "Unless you told them, of course," Minos said, his tone silky and sharp-edged.

"And why would I do that? I've invested a lot of time and money into this operation," Harper snapped. "I'm not about to watch it all go to hell simply because some random civilian recognizes my face."

He poured himself another drink. "My man offered you a face scarf and caftan. You turned him down."

Minos walked over to a nearby couch and settled back into the low, red cushions.

Harper eyed the man, annoyed when the Al Asheera leader didn't remove his scarf. "Keeping up this charade to the end?"

"I find that it's better for my...health, to let my skills build my reputation. One doesn't need a face to establish credibility. Correct?" Minos asked.

"I'd prefer to know whom I am dealing with—"

"Then we're done." Minos rose from his seat. "All deals are off."

"I said I would prefer it—I didn't say it was necessary, damn it."

Both understood the general had just retreated. Red flushed his cheeks. He did not like being on the defensive. But he needed this business taken care of.

"Then I owe you an apology," Minos said easily, but his eyes remained narrow, unyielding. "I misunderstood. Since we are in agreement with the boundaries of our partnership, we may continue."

"My point exactly," Harper responded tersely. "We have wasted enough time."

"Please have a seat." Minos waved to the closest velvet straight-back chair. "My men told me that you have brought the equipment."

"Yes. General Trygg needs it delivered tomorrow,"

Harper replied. "Make sure it is not damaged in the transportation. It's fragile and expensive equipment."

"And the other part of our transaction?"

"I have it here." Harper opened his briefcase on the table. Slowly, he turned the briefcase around until Minos saw its contents. "And three million in bearer bonds."

"For Booker McKnight, Sandra Haddad and Riorden Trygg dead," Minos murmured. "That's quite a bounty for three people."

"Do we have a deal?" Senator Harper handed Minos the piece of paper. "These are the coordinates to his camp."

"That leaves McKnight and Sandra Haddad."

"Chances are if you find Trygg, you will find McKnight and Omar's daughter," Harper snapped. "Trygg is hunting them down."

"He is that close?"

"Close enough," Harper replied. "Trygg is planning on moving his laboratory. Very soon. If that happens, you might not be able to track him."

"Move?"

"He's built his lab in the belly of the airbus we managed to acquire for him," Harper explained. "I didn't think the son of a bitch could pull it off, but he did. He plans on dumping the CIRCADIAN on Taer."

"He wants to wipe out the royal family?"

"He wants to decimate them, along with most of

the country," Harper corrected. "And frankly, I don't care if he does or not. Just so long as you take care of him soon. That's our deal, Minos."

"Yes, General. We have a deal." Minos paused, thinking.

"Who knows, Minos? If you play your cards right, once Trygg hits Taer with the CIRCADIAN, there might be enough left for you to finally have the country for the Al Asheera."

"You can't rule the dead, Senator," Minos murmured. He took a short sip of his whiskey. "What about Omar Haddad?"

Harper's eyes went cold. "I am meeting with him in a few hours."

"A meeting?"

"More like a conversation about old times," Harper corrected. "Don't worry about Omar. I'll take care of him."

"He is not a man who is easily taken care of," Minos pointed out. He placed his drink on a nearby table. "And he, like you, is a father who will stop at nothing to avenge his daughter."

Chapter Thirteen

They traveled most of the day until the heat of the sun forced them to seek shade.

After taking a small break to relieve her bladder, Sandra settled cross-legged on a nearby boulder, closed her eyes and listened.

The wind kicked and howled across the desert floor, stirring sand, loose scrub...and memories.

Its restlessness touched something in her, made her feel connected to the desert more than any-thing—or anyone—could.

She spent many hours sitting on top of the boulders, when the need to be alone became too much.

One time, when she was no more than ten or eleven years of age, Bari joined her. "I see you up here on your perch, day after day. What are you thinking about, little bird?"

"Daydreams mostly," she said softly. "I imagine my wishes are caught up in the desert winds and taken across the sands."

"And where does the Sahara take your dreams?" he asked gently.

Sandra shrugged, not ready to share something so personal. Instead she said, "Aunt Theresa used to tell me that the Sahara was a beautiful woman filled with magic and emotion. Do you think she was right?"

Sadness creased the corners of her uncle's eyes, deepened the brown to a black, mournful and lackluster.

Theresa Bazan had been murdered only a few months before.

Sandra's older brother, Andon, was taken several years earlier than Theresa. Both had died at the hands of the Al Asheera.

While Sandra was too young to remember her brother, she knew and loved her aunt.

"Oh, yes." Bari studied the horizon. "A beautiful woman, full of mischief and surprises."

"Mischief?" Sandra smiled.

"And danger," Bari warned. "Don't ever forget that, Sandra."

"But only to those who don't respect her," Sandra argued. "Even so, the danger adds a sense of adventure. Doesn't it?"

Bari laughed. "You are loyal to the land, little bird."

"Not the land, Uncle. My home."

Bari placed his arms around her shoulder and

gathered her close. "My Theresa would have agreed with you."

"I miss her, too, Uncle. I miss her so much." Sandra was close to her mother, but in a different way. Unlike Sandra's mother, who went from her father's home to her marriage with Omar, Theresa Bazan had traveled the world. She'd been independent, a world-renowned Nobel Prize–winning photographer.

As a Christian, she'd been unable to marry Bari, a royal. So she'd lived with Bari without marriage, and later had given birth to Quamar.

Bari loved her, too. Enough that he'd given up his throne to travel the desert with her. Raise their son together. Until she died. Then Bari raised their son alone.

"She loved you, little bird," Bari murmured. "She was the one who called you that first, you know. She said that you reminded her of a small bird caught in a cage, relentlessly fluttering her wings, but never quite free."

Tears pricked the back of her eyes. "She said that?"

"Yes," Bari replied and patted her knee. "But it's up to you to prove whether she is right or not. My Theresa never agreed with society's rules."

From that day, her uncle always made camp near rocks. Over the years, it remained a private understanding between them. She loved Bari for that and so much more.

"Are you okay?" Sandra started, coming abruptly back to the present.

Booker stood at her feet, his gaze narrowed, studying her face.

"I'm fine. Just resting."

"Rest somewhere out of the sun," he ordered. "The last thing we need to deal with is a doctor with sunstroke."

"I wasn't planning to stay out here for more than a few minutes." Sandra slipped off the rock and dusted off her caftan. "Besides, I'm properly covered."

"Come over here."

Booker found a few sticks. He stripped out of his caftan, tied it to the poles and created a small lean-to for them to rest beneath.

"I'll be back with some food," he told her. "After we eat, we need to rest while the sun is hot. We'll travel in a few hours."

As if on cue, her stomach growled. It had been two solid days since she had more than just some cheese and sweet bread.

Sandra sat beneath the lean-to, enjoyed the breeze against her face, the warm sand at her feet.

This is where she belonged. This was worth fighting for.

Booker returned a moment later, brown bag in

hand. "Dinner. Your favorite." He dug into the bag and pulled out a jar. "Bread and peanut butter."

"Peanut butter?" A wide grin spread across her lips.

"Seems Yesemie shares your obsession for this stuff. I found a secret stash in the back of his jeep." A moment later he held up a loaf of bread.

"How nice of him."

"Didn't find anything else but some water."

"When you work in a warehouse, why do you need supplies in your car?" Sandra joked, knowing they wouldn't get far with minimal supplies.

As if reading her thoughts, Booker tipped up her chin. Gave her a soft kiss on the nose. "Don't worry, Doc. We'll figure it out."

"I know." She smiled, holding the moment in her heart.

With a wink, he stepped away. "You grab the bread." He settled next her, unscrewed the jar top and unsheathed his knife. "He also left us a few machine guns and explosives."

"Lucky us." Sandra laughed, then tore off a big chunk of the bread and held it up.

Booker went still for a second, enjoying the soft, feminine sound as it rolled through her chest, caught on her smile.

He scooped out some peanut butter and spread it across the bread in her hand, deliberately avoiding the touch of their fingertips.

Greedy, she sank her teeth into it and closed her eyes. She ran her tongue over her lips to catch any extra.

"Doc?"

Her eyes opened. Booker stared at her mouth; desire burned hot and pure in his eyes.

"If you keep eating like that, you're not going to finish," he warned, his voice low.

A ripple of feminine pride and excitement trickled through her. For the first time in a long time, a few bars of her birdcage broke away.

"Sorry," she said and almost meant it. Covering a smile, she set her bread carefully in her lap and reached over to him.

He jumped just a bit at the contact of her fingers on his.

"Let me." She took the knife from him. Before you hurt yourself, she wanted to add, but didn't.

"You know, there has always been a question I wanted to ask you," she mentioned instead. She spread the peanut butter, folded over the bread and handed it to him.

"Why not?"

"Why not what?"

"Why didn't you ever ask, Doc?"

"Seriously?" she scoffed. "We had so many secrets between us, Booker, I'd trip over them on my way from our bed to the bathroom."

Booker didn't argue her point. Instead he took a

bite of bread, chewed for a moment. "There never seemed to be a good time to work on us."

"We slept together, but we weren't intimate," Sandra remarked. "No hand-holding. No quiet, romantic evenings."

But with no resentment. Just too many walls. Too much responsibility. They were entrenched in their own paths.

They were…her parents, she realized, surprised. Her father buried in his career, her mother in her duties as his wife.

"And you want to know why," he stated.

"No, actually. I think I figured that one out myself," Sandra answered truthfully. Somehow her inner radar gravitated toward a man she was comfortable with. A man driven by his past. While responsible and reliable, he was void of emotion. No, she corrected, a man able to suppress and control his emotions.

A man like her father.

"I always wondered how you got your first name."

"It's a family name," he replied, surprised. "Booker was my mother's maiden name. She came from an affluent background. Her family was big on making sure all the descendants of the women carried their name."

"Booker?" Sandra frowned. "As in Francis Booker, heir to Booker Enterprises?"

"The same."

Booker Enterprises was old money. Mayflower money. Been around longer than the Rockefellers. Most known for oil. They had their fingers in every major technical and urban industry.

"Wow." Sandra blew out the word. "But I thought... Quamar told me once..."

"That I came from a poor background?"

She nodded.

"That's because I did. On my father's side."

"Your father?"

"His name was Malcolm McKnight. My mother met my father on a drill site she was visiting with her father." Booker took another bite of his sandwich and paused for a moment. "At the time, my grandfather, Samuel Booker, was interested in investing in oil."

"Samuel as in Sam the horse?"

"Yes. He bought the rights to a drilling site my father worked on."

"That's when your father met your mother."

Booker nodded. "They were sixteen. Just kids. But they fell in love on sight. The trouble was that my mother was an only child with only her father left to raise her. My grandmother had died when my mother was young. My grandfather had wanted my mom to marry into their circle."

"She was a bargaining chip?"

"No." Booker shook his head. "My grandfather loved my mother and wanted only the best for her.

But when my grandfather forbade the marriage, she ran away with my dad."

Booker's jaw tightened, holding back the resentment that his words, didn't...couldn't disguise.

"My grandfather was furious. He disowned my mother the moment he found out. Then he proceeded to buy up as many oil companies he could and black-balled my father from the fields. Only those who knew nothing of my mother's family or the story or disliked my grandfather gave my father a job.

"We didn't have health care. When I was ten, my mom caught pneumonia. My dad wanted to go to my grandfather and ask for help to pay for medical care but my mom made him promise not to. She died the next day, in my father's arms."

"Promise or not, he should have tried—"

"My father loved her until the day he died. I was eighteen at the time." Booker tossed his sandwich away, wiped his hands on his thighs. "He got caught in the backlash of loose steel cable. It ripped him in two."

"Booker, I'm so sorry." Her hand automatically went to his shoulder.

"It happened a long time ago, Doc." Booker shrugged off her hand, shifted back onto his elbows and stretched out his legs.

She let her hand drop to her lap.

"The funny thing is, he only lived a few minutes and was in a tremendous amount of pain," Booker continued. "Yet he died with my mother's name on his lips and a smile on his face. It was as if he'd welcomed death because he'd be with her again. He loved her that much."

"Their love must have been incredible. And so tragic," Sandra murmured. "It reminds me of my uncle Bari and my aunt Theresa."

"The irony is, a few years ago, my grandfather took ill. His lawyers showed up on my doorstep. My grandfather wanted me back in the family. I closed the door in their face. And haven't seen him since."

"Is he still living?"

"Oh, yes," Booker stated, his frown deepening. "He's ninety-three and a stubborn old bastard."

Like his grandson, Sandra mused, sure that Booker wouldn't appreciate the comparison.

"He sends me letters. I return them unopened."

So many secrets. So much distance.

"All of them?" Instinctively, she knew he wasn't telling her the whole story. Why wouldn't he just throw the letters away? Why take the time to send the letters back?

Because the old man was his only family. At least sending the letters back maintained some kind of connection.

For the first time she understood—the distance wasn't only with her. He maintained the same detachment with everyone.

Booker's whole family had died on him. His mother, his father. Emily and their baby. His men.

"Yes. I sent every one of the letters back." Booker nodded toward her sandwich. "Eat your lunch. You're going to need the energy."

"Doctor." She pointed at her bag by her side. "Remember?" Still, she took a bite of her food. But this time the peanut butter tasted more like the sand around her feet.

"In my experience, doctors are the worst offenders," Booker retorted.

"How many doctors do you know?"

"Just one. Isn't that enough?" he teased.

"Funny." With a smirk, she tossed her sandwich away, daring him to make a comment.

Instead, he closed his eyes, taking a moment to enjoy the easy camaraderie they'd stumbled upon.

She looked out over the desert, enjoying the simple blend of the cloudless sky and endless sand. "One thing Trygg did for me. He gave me a reason to come home after the trial."

Booker opened one eye, saw the relaxed features, the quiet, ironic smile across her lips.

"You want to tell me what happened?"

"You've seen the file." She stretched out her legs and dusted the crumbs off her pants.

"I'd like your version."

"All right." He'd opened up about his family, she thought. She needed to do the same. "After I graduated from college, I got a job in Washington, D.C., working on a military research project under the direct report of General Trygg."

"CIRCADIAN?"

"Yes," Sandra said, frowning. "It worked at a rate of a thousand times faster then the average healthy body can heal."

"Super Soldiers," Booker grunted. "Trygg's specialty."

"Exactly," Sandra agreed. "Although I didn't know it at the time. My father had been informed of the research opportunity shortly after I left college."

"Who told him?"

"He never said." Sandra paused, thinking. "I interviewed with several individuals. Several or all might have talked with my father."

"Including Trygg?"

"Trygg, Senator Harper, Kate MacAlister," she admitted. "President Mercer."

Booker stiffened in surprise. "You interviewed with Jonathon Mercer?"

"For over an hour. In his private quarters," Sandra explained. "I remember being surprised at the extent of his knowledge of CIRCADIAN."

Booker wasn't, but said nothing. Instead, he snagged a bottle of water from the brown bag. Took a long swallow. More to cover his anger than for thirst. "Your father's social circle includes some high-powered company."

He offered Sandra the bottle.

She swallowed a small amount and handed it back to him. "As a young man, my father studied in the States and graduated at the top of his class. He was recruited into government work almost immediately. I don't know the projects, of course—they were all top secret. But he maintained his contacts even after he'd left the government and returned to Taer."

When Booker remained silent, she said, "I know what you're thinking."

"No, you don't," he responded evenly, keeping his features deliberately blank. Omar Haddad had been a government operative long after he'd returned to Taer.

"You're thinking somehow if my father is involved, the reason might lie in one of those top secret projects he was involved in years ago."

"All right," Booker lied. "I have to admit it's logical."

"I would have pursued the job without my father's help. I had my own reasons for wanting this serum to work, but I needed the funds."

"What reason?"

"It's personal."

"Too personal to share."

"I've lost family members, Booker," she answered slowly, still not willing to trust him with the information on her brother Andon.

She placed her hand on his arm for a brief second. "I can't help believing I would save those I have left."

Booker nodded, understanding. "How did the project get away from you?"

"Eventually I made a breakthrough and Trygg fired my boss, and placed me as the lead researcher. What I didn't know at the time was that he altered my reports to suit his needs. Omitting information, falsifying test results."

"Who did he fire?"

"Kate MacAlister-D'Amato," she said quietly.

"Why?"

"Kate questioned every decision Trygg made," Sandra stated. "And she had connections to back her up."

"Obviously, that made Trygg nervous."

Sandra snorted. "Trygg doesn't get nervous. He got angry. And then he got rid of her."

"He would've killed her. You know that, right?" Booker asked.

"Now I do," Sandra replied. "He couldn't easily, though, because she was so well connected."

"Trygg brought in Lewis Pitman?"

"Yes," Sandra said. "Kate tried to convince me to leave also, but I was Trygg's shining star."

"You were young," Booker observed. "Too young to lead a top secret, high-priority research project."

"I was naive and full of myself," she corrected, her self-disgust palpable. "Kate went to work on another project, and I continued working on the cell reconstruction serum. You know the rest."

"And Trygg?"

"I didn't know at the time, but Trygg couldn't have been happier."

"Fifty men died," Booker said grimly.

Sandra nodded. "Yes. Because of something I created."

"That's where you're wrong, Doc. Trygg is an unbalanced killer with a god complex," Booker corrected her, the edge of his words cutting the air between them. "Those men died because Trygg murdered them."

"Why is Trygg afraid of you, Booker?"

"Trygg decided to let me live. He sent me on a wild-goose chase. I know him. There isn't a day that goes by that he doesn't regret that decision." Booker shoved the water back into the backpack. "And when I catch up with him, he's not going back to prison. I'm sending him straight to hell."

Chapter Fourteen

Pitman followed Jim down the circular stairway to the main floor of the lab. "Is everything satisfactory, Doctor?"

"Almost," Lewis replied, pleased.

The lab ran the length of the plane. Hundreds of square feet of fitted steel and white tile, Plexiglas and state-of-the-art technology.

"The only thing missing are the cylinders," Pitman advised him. "Have you located Sandra Haddad?"

"Not yet."

"Do you know where she is at least?"

"We know who she's with," Jim answered.

"Who?"

"Booker McKnight."

Pitman stopped at the base of the stairs, blocking Jim. "Senator Harper's son-in-law?"

"Yes," Jim acknowledged. "But he will be taken care of soon."

"You realize it is harder dealing with a man bent on revenge than one who just wants more money?"

"I understand the man more than you think, Lewis. Booker McKnight was more than just military, or loyal. Those men trusted Booker and he let them down. They were his responsibility, his family," Jim replied. "I'd be surprised if Booker didn't go after Trygg. Hell, I'd do the same in his shoes."

"I'm not talking about his men, Colonel. I'm talking about his wife, Emily," Pitman stated bluntly. "I told Trygg killing Harper's daughter along with his men was an unnecessary risk."

"The general always weighs the options," Jim prodded, keeping his voice even, his expression blank. "Emily Harper's death was unavoidable. She snuck on the base to see Booker without authorization."

"Unavoidable? Trygg knew that Emily was on the base," Pitman scoffed. "How long have you served under General Trygg? That man doesn't do anything without a purpose."

"What do you mean?" Jim turned, backed Pitman up against the stairs.

Pitman's eyes widened. "I understand that circumstance made Emily's death a last-minute decision, but it wasn't unavoidable." Fear made his voice shake. "When Trygg received the call up in the airplane that Emily crashed the gates, we hadn't dropped the cylinder yet. I told him he needed more time to think it through. That killing Harper's daughter would bring attention to our operation. He disagreed."

Jim's jaw tightened. The trouble was he couldn't trust Pitman. The man was a rat; he'd kill his own children to save his skin.

"General Trygg understood the importance of the situation," Jim said flatly, but was unable to dismiss the doctor's theory. He stepped back, giving them both room—and Jim time to think over this new information.

Pitman cleared his throat, used the moment to gain his composure. "Don't get me wrong, Colonel. I agree with Trygg's reasoning. Those who died did so for a good cause whether they knew it or not. Harper's daughter was just another casualty of war," Pitman acknowledged. "I'd just prefer it if Booker McKnight wasn't lurking somewhere in the shadows."

RIORDEN TRYGG STOOD at the opening of his tent and sipped his coffee, enjoying the bite against his tongue.

It didn't matter, jungle humidity or desert heat, Trygg drank his coffee strong and hot.

Harper had pulled some strings on the Hill, managed to acquire a mobile electromagnetic pulse emitter. Or what the higher-ups called an EMP Transportable.

The senator said it would be delivered today,

Trygg thought. He glanced at the sun at the top of the sky. Today was half-over.

Rivet guns punched the air, shaking the earth, sending a lizard scurrying over his feet.

In less than twenty-four hours, the airbus would be a fully operational mobile laboratory for the CIRCADIAN.

Trygg wanted the plane secure, the army tank secure. They'd gutted the inside, filled it with the necessary equipment, but it was not worth the effort or the money if all it would take was one missile to bring her down.

The EMP, while limited in range, would emit enough electromagnetic pulse to fry most electronic instruments in a five-mile radius. Including surface-to-air missiles or fighter jets.

Trygg took another sip of coffee. From his position, he watched the men maneuver on the scaffolds beneath the netting. He'd wait a few hours, until the heat from the sun had worn off, before he inspected the day's results. A necessary duty, with pleasing results.

Trygg was more than satisfied with the progress on the airplane. But then again, he expected nothing less than top results from those he hired.

Jim had recruited the best. Promised them money beyond their dreams.

The fact they'd never live to see their payoff lay easy on Trygg's conscience.

Sacrifices had to be made for the greater good.

Lewis stepped down from the plane, giving orders. Two men followed him to the plane's underbelly, where the bay door stood open.

Trygg didn't trust Pitman. But one didn't have to trust a man to appreciate his usefulness.

The wind picked up, making the walls of the tent shudder. Trygg caught the scent of hamburger and grease from the mess tents a few hundred yards away.

Lunchtime soon.

He had forty men supporting him in this campaign. More than enough.

"From the satisfied look on your face, the mission is going as planned." The voice spoke from outside the tent, just beyond his shoulder, catching Trygg off guard.

"Minos," he greeted casually. But the hair bristled at the base of Trygg's neck, and irritation pulled between his shoulders. The Al Asheera leader moved like a ghost. "This is an unexpected surprise."

"Thought I'd see how the project was coming along."

"We're on schedule," Trygg answered, his annoyance barely contained. He took in the other man's scarf-covered features, the desert garb.

"And the cylinders?"

"All aspects of this mission are being handled," Trygg replied stiffly. "To your satisfaction, I believe."

Trygg turned on his heel and walked back into his tent.

"I have no complaints." Minos followed, chuckling. He took in the massive desk, the leather straight-back chairs, the dining table complete with china and a fruit bowl, brimming with red apples, ripe oranges. "You live well, General."

"I live civilized," Trygg corrected. He placed his coffee on his desk and took his hat from a nearby coat stand. "You should try it sometime."

"It's not easy for me. I'm nothing more than a paid killer most times," Minos replied slyly. "In fact, I was just paid one million dollars by Senator Harper to kill you."

Trygg froze for a moment, his hat never making it to his head. "May I ask why?"

"I don't care," Minos replied. "So I didn't ask. Not many men can manage three million dollars in bearer bonds as payment."

He acknowledged Minos's statement with a short nod before settling the hat on his head. "The amount doesn't mean anything to Keith. He's from old money."

"It means quite a bit to me." Minos tsk-tsked. "Did you two have a fight, General?"

"He might not have agreed with some of my past decisions," Trygg acknowledged with deliberate vagueness. "Did you agree to take the contract?"

"I took his money. But we didn't shake on it."

Minos shrugged. "I'll take care of Harper so he stays out of your way. That was our deal."

"Not all of it. You have the EMP?"

"Yes. My men left it just beyond the East Ridge. I didn't want them accidentally mistaken for the enemy and shot during the transfer."

"You don't trust me."

"Trusting you wasn't part of our deal," Minos replied. He grabbed a red apple from the fruit bowl, tossed it in his hand. "Do you have McKnight contained?"

"I'll tell my men to move the emitter." Trygg stepped out into the open, caught the scent of moisture in the air. "We're in for a storm."

"Sahara storms are more common than most think." Minos glanced up at the sky. Dark clouds swirled over the hilltops; electricity charged the air. "A hint of what is to come maybe?"

"For whom?"

"Depends on where a person is at the time," Minos quipped. "One thing for sure, Harper may have stopped Cain MacAlister from sending men over here the other day."

"You heard about that?"

Minos shrugged. "You still have a major problem on your hands, General."

"And that would be?"

"King Jarek and Quamar. I wouldn't underestimate them. Or their men."

"I don't," Trygg replied, his tone razor-sharp. "That's why I hired you. To take care of them. After all, who would know them better than their oldest enemy?"

"Who indeed?" Minos acknowledged, then glanced at the men standing guard over the plane. "By the way, your men have holes on your perimeter. You need to shore them up, or you'll be done before this thing starts."

"Where?" Trygg turned toward the plane. When he got no answer, he turned back, then swore.

He stood alone.

"THIS IS IT." Booker parked the jeep at the base of the mountain. He leaned over the wheel and peered through the rain-spattered windshield. Fifty feet of rock and cliff surrounded them, divided by a ravine less than twenty feet wide.

"The ravine is too dangerous for the jeep. If this storm picks up, we'll get washed away in a flash flood."

The air, thick with moisture and hints of electricity, churned up the dust and grit, spattered it with drops of water.

"We don't have much time, Booker." Sandra pushed open the door, struggled against the strong gusts of wind and pelting rain.

Booker left the headlights on, then met her in front

of the beams. Within moments, thunder cracked, the skies opened up and the storm broke free.

"We need to move to higher ground now," he yelled over the downpour. "Before this wind kicks up more debris."

"Here!" Booker shouted over the clamor of the storm. He pointed to a crevice off the ravine. In the dim light she made out the steep path to a higher ridge.

Lightning flashed. On its heels came another crack of thunder. Minutes passed and rain continued to pound the earth with heavy fists. Smooth surfaces grew treacherous; the wind whipped scrub and rocks into a frenzy.

They reached the twenty-foot ledge in unspoken urgency. The rain continued to rage. Water poured from the shadows and crevices into the ravine below.

Suddenly, the wind drowned under a muffled roar. Booker swore. "The water is coming! We aren't high enough!"

They searched the side of the canyon, finding nothing but slick walls. Booker tugged Sandra's hand, pulled her blindly into the shadows.

Without warning the wall broke free into a crevice that turned into a wide path up through the ravine.

"Booker!" Sandra yanked back on his hand. He turned, saw the narrow path that led up through some boulders.

"Go!" he yelled over the roar.

Sandra scrambled up through the rocks; sharp edges bit and scraped her palms.

She squeezed between two boulders, came out onto a path that led to a higher ledge. Ten feet higher. Quickly, she scrambled, praying Booker stayed close.

The wall of water hit. Rolling and pitching, the waves threw scrub and rocks, tumbling them like dice.

The water caught at Sandra's clothes. Booker slammed his knife into a nearby crevice, anchoring the blade. He gripped the handle until his knuckles whitened, pinning Sandra between him and the wall.

Water rushed around them, slammed them against the stone, washed out the dirt beneath their feet.

"Hold on to me!" Booker yelled through the blast, gripping the knife, gripping Sandra.

She locked her arms around his waist—praying for the first time in many years.

Moments later, the water fell away, became a trickle at their feet. But the wind whipped, the rain poured.

Booker stepped away. Sandra's muscles shook with fatigue, and she knew fear.

She eased away from the wall, her body stiff, her skin on fire from cuts and bruises.

But still alive.

Uprooted scrub lay snagged around the serrated rocks with only puddles left from the flood.

"That was easy enough," she joked weakly, her teeth chattering. Her hand flexed on the strap of her medical bag, but for the first time she didn't care about it getting lost.

Her clothes clung to her, cold and wet. Strands of hair stuck to her cheeks, clung to the back and sides of her neck.

"You all right?" He gripped her shoulders, rubbed some warmth into her icy limbs.

"Yes." She clenched her jaw, kept her teeth from knocking together, locked her knees and willed the strength back into her legs.

"We can't stop here. There are only a few more hours of sunlight. It's best if we go higher, find a cave and rest for the night," he explained gently. Without warning, he tipped his forehead until it touched hers. "Are you up for it, Doc?"

"Don't be nice to me now, Booker. Or I'll fall apart," she whispered back. Tears pricked at her eyes; she blinked hard against the sting. "Just get me somewhere safe, so we can rest. Okay?"

"Okay." He interlaced his fingers with hers, squeezed just a bit to give her back the strength she needed. "Watch the rocks. The flood softened the terrain making it unstable."

An hour later, they found a cave. The entrance stood seven feet high and four feet wide, with a lip over the ground that hid a flat, earth-packed floor.

A scattering of rocks and a fairly large boulder littered the space inside.

"Here." She reached into her bag and pulled out a mini flashlight.

Booker thumbed it on and flashed it inside of the cave. "Stay close."

She followed him, keeping her arms crossed, her body tight against the chill that settled in the night air.

The scent of damp earth and stale air tickled her nose. The pattering of rain grew, echoing off the wall.

"The storm's picking up again."

"We're good. The flood level won't reach this high." Booker stopped abruptly, swore when she bumped into him and felt the icy skin of her hand against his arm.

They had nothing to stay warm. No blanket, no dry clothes. "Do you still have my lighter?"

Booker explored the cave, found dried branches and scrub behind the farthest rock. "There's enough kindling here for a small fire. We can keep it going most of the night." Within a few short minutes, flames glowed and flickered.

When she sighed—a trusting sigh that almost brought him to his knees—Booker gathered her close, tucked her head beneath his chin.

"I almost lost you." He hadn't meant to say the words. Hadn't even realized he'd thought them until they'd passed his lips. But it was there, in the pounding of his heart, the trembling of his fingers, the raw need to protect.

Slowly, she tilted her head back, found the glitter of truth in his blue irises.

Years of questions, fear and distrust all broke loose under a tidal wave of understanding and tenderness.

"Not tonight." She lifted her chin, brushed her lips against his.

The taste of honey and spice slid over his tongue, caught at the back of his throat.

"Not tonight." His fingers threaded her dampened tresses, cupped the sides of her face.

Desire spread through his body, a hot lava that infused his limbs, rushed through his veins.

"Heat." Sandra curled farther into him, made him tremble. "We need more heat."

"Any more and I'll burst into flames."

"I'll save you," she whispered. Her mouth moved over his neck, nibbled his jaw. Then she was kissing him. Hot, moist, openmouthed kisses that had the blood rushing from his head, pooling just under his gut. The movement made him hard, made him groan.

He tried to push her away, but instead his arms tightened around her. His hands delved into the soft folds of her hair, let the damp locks catch around his fingers.

"I have a better way to keep us warm," she whispered, her voice raspy, urgent.

"I think…" His arm slipped under her knees, lifted her up into his arms. He settled them both on the ground, with her on top, chest to chest, hips bumping hips. "…it might take a while."

Her hand snaked down between them, stroked the hard length of him, unsnapped his pants. "It might take all night." Booker let out his breath in a long hiss.

Electricity crackled the air, skimmed over her skin. This time it wasn't the storm outside, but the one between them.

"I don't think we're going anywhere." Her hands found the bottom edge of her shirt, yanked it over her arms and head.

His mouth latched on to her nipple, and his tongue rubbed the hard point through the thin cloth of her bra.

Sandra leaned back, let his hands catch her at her ribs, held her in place while he nuzzled, nibbled and stroked.

Her fingers curled in his hair, pulled him closer.

The damp smell of her skin, her hair, enveloped him, drove his senses to a fever pitch, his body to the precipice of his control.

Then she was kissing him, using tongue and teeth, fanning the heat into a firestorm of desire.

Booker broke under the onslaught. His arms clamped on to her, making her finish what she started.

Needing her to…

His hands swept down her back, over her pants. Suddenly, they were off and his fingers stroked until her skin burned, her nerves jumped.

He nudged her legs apart. She rose above him, the fire at her back, the muted hues surrounding her, flickering over her skin, softening the shadows, turning her into an exotic creature of the night.

He groaned, locked his hands on her hips and buried his arousal at the apex of her thighs.

"Now, Booker."

Her fingers fluttered, finding his zipper, tugging and pulling with jerky movements—tormented by the raging desire.

His fingers delved into the moist center between her thighs, touching, stroking until she writhed with pleasure.

She raised up, arched, stretched and, with trembling limbs, accepted.

SANDRA AWAKENED SLOWLY. More from the sudden chill of air over her back than from the soft rustle of branches.

She blinked hard. The shadows shifted; her eyes adjusted.

The storm raged, battering the cave entrance.

When she shivered, Booker was there, pressed up against her back, his arms around her.

For the first time in a long time, Sandra felt safe.

"I just added more branches to the fire," Booker whispered, his breath warm and moist against her ear.

When she shivered, he tightened his hold. His teeth nibbled her ear. Goose bumps tripped down her spine and settled at the base. She nestled into the crook of his arm.

"Go back to sleep. We need to get some rest while we can." He slid his arms under her. Slowly he pulled her on top of his chest, let her legs tangle with his.

"Rest?"

Sandra kissed his chest, settled her head just over his heart, finding the steady beat reassuring, the tickle of hair against her cheek soothing.

"How far are we from the cylinders, Doc?"

She'd known the question was coming, expected it. Sad that their moment had been so brief. "I'm not quite sure. Maybe a half day's ride up the ravine."

"You're not sure?"

She could've just stalled, waited until he was distracted, but suddenly Sandra was tired of all the secrets. The walls that still remained steadfast between them.

"I have to check my map, Booker," she said quietly.

"What map?" His muscles stiffened into granite planes, leaving her skin cold, her heart aching.

"The one I made five years ago. It shows the location of the cylinders." She shifted back, needing some space, readying herself for the rejection.

Slowly, he rolled her back onto the ground, then looked down on her.

"It was an insurance policy in case something happened to me. I know his men were loyal and hadn't been rounded up after he'd been sent to Leavenworth. Especially Colonel Rayo. He's Trygg's right-hand man—"

"I know who Rayo is, damn it."

Sandra saw it then, what she missed. The cold anger in the blue eyes. A familiar sadness swept through her chest, making it tight, leaving her heart aching. Nothing had changed. Would change.

"Where is this map?" Booker demanded. "In your medical pack, right?"

"In the lining," she admitted, but didn't flinch when his fingers tightened on her shoulder. Instead she tossed him the bag. Watched him rip it open. "That's why I never left it behind. I couldn't risk trying to remember. If I had forgotten…"

Booker stared at the information on the cloth. He let out a sting of curses.

Her chin came up, defiant. "I did what I needed to do, Booker. And I don't regret it."

"When were you going to let me know?"

"Now," she snapped. "Or did you miss the confession a minute ago?"

Before he could answer she added, "You have no right to be angry, damn it. How much have you kept from me, McKnight?"

Booker forced himself to let her go. He grabbed his clothes and tugged them on. The dampness did little to cool the heat of his anger.

"I have every right," Booker bit out. "I wanted you safe."

"I told you before. I'm safest with you."

"No, you're not!" His tone was low, the words terse. "I followed you here, Doc. Four years ago! I didn't do that because I was told to, or because I was concerned, or even because I was madly in love with you. I followed you four years ago because I knew that Trygg would eventually escape from prison. He had too many contacts, too much backing behind him not to. I studied his profile, damn it. I knew."

"You followed me because of Trygg?" She stood, feeling too vulnerable sitting on the ground naked. With quick, jerky movements, she grabbed her clothes off the boulder, tugged them on over her bra and panties.

"Once he escaped, who do you think he'd come after?"

"Me," she admitted. "So all of this…" She pointed

her finger back and forth between them, not able to finish. Not when his face hardened, his gaze swept over her semi-naked state.

"You were my bait, Doc. Nothing more."

She'd paid a high price for what she'd done, what she'd risked for CIRCADIAN. Her family. Booker. Love.

But this? Her knees buckled. Only sheer willpower and pride kept her upright.

She zipped up her pants, pulled her shirt over her head.

He'd used her.

He'd slept with her. And used her.

Sandra widened her stance to keep her feet under her, the mortification at bay.

Her fingers shook, but she forced herself to ignore them and slipped on her caftan.

"Be ready in five minutes." The command was sharp, his features set in granite.

He had no right to be angry. He'd *used* her.

Bait for Trygg.

Then why was she still standing here, damn it? The thought ricocheted from the back of her mind.

More than once they had faced Trygg's men. Each time he could have used her by informing Trygg's men he'd negotiate. But he didn't. He killed them or left them behind. No negotiation.

He wanted the cylinders and her home.

A person can't be bait when they're placed out of harm's way.

Chapter Fifteen

The phone vibrated the nightstand.

President Jonathon Mercer ignored the light switch on the lamp and grabbed the receiver instead. He glanced at the digital clock. Four in the morning.

In his eighth year of presidency, he'd long become accustomed to calls at all hours of the night. Especially on his private line.

"Mercer."

His wife shifted onto her elbow, her blue eyes questioning, more curious than startled.

"Mr. President, it is Omar Haddad."

"One moment."

Jon patted his wife's hip, telling her to go back to sleep. She nodded, gave him a soft kiss on his cheek and turned over.

He slid from the bed and stepped onto the balcony. The air stirred around him. He noted a few of the Secret Service doing their job, but none were in earshot.

"I can talk now, Omar. What the hell is going on? Why haven't you returned my calls?"

"I've been a little busy, Jon, locating my daughter."

"I told you that I had a man on the inside keeping an eye on her."

"I hope that man is Booker McKnight because he's the one who has her."

"Who told you that?"

"Jarek informed me after a visit he received from Cain MacAlister. The king assured me that McKnight would keep my daughter safe. As if I would believe that nonsense," Omar scoffed.

"Jarek met with Cain?" Jon clarified, the anger immediate but controlled. A five-year operation suddenly at risk.

"Yes," Omar answered.

His temper snapped then. "Without notifying me first?"

"The last time I checked, Mr. President, the King of Taer wasn't obligated to share that kind of information with you."

"Cain MacAlister is." The Director of Labyrinth reported directly to the President of the United States.

"Jarek considers this a domestic problem. Trygg is in his country. It makes him Jarek's problem, not yours."

Jonathon let it go. For the moment. "Where was Sandra and Booker's last known location?"

"Tourlay. Until they blew up a warehouse, stole a vehicle and left the city. I've been with Bari, trying to locate them through village contacts," Omar continued. "All I know is that they are somewhere on the run in the desert."

"Bari knows the desert and its people," Jon reasoned out loud. "And he hasn't found them?"

"Not yet."

Jon swore silently. "Omar. I will contact my man and get the status on your daughter. She will be fine."

"You gave me your word, Mr. President, that she'd be safe from Trygg. That is the only reason why I agreed to this situation."

"She will be fine." Jon said a small prayer that he'd be right. "If she is with Booker McKnight, he'll keep her safe."

"Booker has every reason to want her dead," Omar argued. "You and I both know that. If he finds out what I've done—"

"He won't," Jon lied, suspecting Booker already knew. He needed Omar's assistance and the man's focus on the situation. "I understand you and Elizabeth are probably out of your minds with worry. I've been there. But the best thing to do at this point is follow our original plan. Concentrate on that. I'll take whatever precautions necessary to make sure Sandra is kept safe."

"You gave that same promise five years ago—"

"And I will keep that promise, Omar," Jon interrupted. He shifted, uncomfortable with his next sentence. Yet he had no choice. "You have my word."

After a long moment of silence, Omar sighed over the phone. "All right. Two hours. Make sure your man is ready."

"I will," Jon Mercer replied.

"After this, we are what you Americans call *square.* I am no longer in your debt."

"We were square when you gave me your daughter for this project. Now I will be in your debt, Omar." Jon waited for the line to click off, then he punched in another number.

It answered after the first ring. "Cain MacAlister."

"You have exactly twenty minutes to get your butt in my office," Jon snapped. "After that, I'm having you arrested for treason. You got me, MacAlister?"

The silence lasted only a few seconds. Jon knew Cain was weighing his options. "Yes, sir."

Jon hung up.

"It appears as if you and Cain are starting your day early." Shantelle Mercer hugged him from behind. "Do you want me to order up some coffee, *chéri?*"

They both knew Cain was like a son to Jon. Still,

he would not tolerate disloyalty among his ranks. Personal relationships or not.

Jon turned in his wife's arms, seeking comfort. Shantelle Mercer stood just past his shoulder, a small woman with delicate features and a temper that did her French heritage proud.

Jon kissed his wife's forehead. "If I handle this wrong, a young woman will lose her life."

"You are not God, *mi amore*." Shantelle squeezed him slightly, having loved this man all of her life. "You have no control over the choices that others make."

He thought of his daughter Lara, now married to Cain's brother Ian. "I might not be God but I am still a father."

"Well, then, I guess that means Sandra Haddad will be fine."

Jon pulled back, frowned. Obviously, his wife heard more of the conversation than he'd thought. "Why do you say that?"

"Because, while you are a wonderful President, Jon, you are an *amazing* father."

"I hope so, my love." Jon gave her another kiss, this time, softly on her lips. "I will take that coffee."

"Give me a few minutes." When Shantelle stepped back into the bedroom, Jon closed the patio door. He punched in one more number on his cell.

This call could not be overheard by anyone.

"Yes?" The one impatient word shot across the private line.

"Why didn't you tell me Booker had Sandra?"

"I told you, Sandra Haddad is in good hands," the man answered. "I never said they were my hands. Booker will take care of her better than I could."

"I don't agree—"

"He is in love with her," the man interrupted. "They have less to worry about when they are together. With me she would have been constantly wondering about him."

Jon didn't agree with the reasoning, but understood this far away there was little he could do.

"All right," Jon replied. "I just received word. You'll make contact in two hours. Is everything in place?"

"Yes, sir," the man answered grimly.

Jon understood. This had been a long time coming. Twenty-five years. "I want that son of a bitch brought down, Sabra."

"That's the plan, Mr. President."

THE PALACE GARDENS HAD taken on a new look with added blooms of roses and lilacs. A touch of Jarek's wife, Queen Sarah's, green thumb, Quamar thought.

Peaceful, beautiful.

The grounds remained silent. No laughter or chatter of the tourists wandering in and out. No children running along the paths.

Security had shut down the tours, shut down the gates against those who did not hold security clearance.

Five days had passed, and still he could not locate his friends.

The weight of his problems shifted between his shoulders.

Quamar stretched against the restlessness. He missed his wife, Anna, and their children. He worried about Sandra.

And Booker, he admitted silently. He had come to like the Texan.

Something whispered past him. The brush of a pant leg against a bush, the soft step of a shoe on the pebbled path.

Quamar reached for his gun and stopped. Cold steel prodded the base of his neck.

"Hello, Quamar." Aaron Sabra's voice drifted over Quamar's shoulder. "Raise your hands slowly until I can see your fingers wiggle."

Quamar brought his hands up to shoulder level but refused to comply with the finger movement.

Aaron Sabra laughed, then stepped to the side of the path, his gun held high, pointed at Quamar's chest. "You have no sense of humor, Bazan."

Quamar glanced down at the other man's leg, immediately noticed the absence of Aaron's limp. "Not bad for a cripple."

"Helped keep me off the radar." Sabra grinned and placed more weight on his bad leg. "You're smarter than your friend Booker."

"Don't count on it," Quamar replied. "Did you injure any of my men when you let yourself in?"

"Not injured enough to require a doctor, if that's what you mean. Most are just taking an unexpected siesta."

"Why should I believe an ex-military convict from Leavenworth?"

Aaron's eyes went cold, flat. "You believe me, or you wouldn't have bothered to ask."

Quamar looked beyond the eyes to the man beneath. He'd known Sabra long before his defection from Labyrinth. Long enough to dismiss the rumors surrounding the man's short stint at Leavenworth.

"Tell me why you are here, Sabra," Quamar stated, deciding to listen.

"I am simply a messenger this time. Requesting assistance from a third party."

"And this third party?" Quamar asked. "Is it someone I know? Because if not, I have some personal matters that need my attention—"

"I want the same answers that you, Jarek and Cain are after, Bazan," Aaron interjected.

"I have no knowledge of what—"

"I heard Cain MacAlister paid you and the king a visit."

"From who?" Quamar's eyebrow rose, but his tone stayed noncommittal.

Aaron ignored the question. "Did they tell you that Trygg had been sent to prison because he killed Booker's men?"

"And if they did?"

"Did they tell you that Booker's wife also died that day?"

Quamar's eyes narrowed on Aaron. "Booker's wife died from complications of a pregnancy. It was in his background check I completed before we hired him."

"That's half the truth," Aaron stated. "Very few are privy to all the details. When I say few, I can count them on one hand."

"And I am supposed to take your word for this?" Quamar demanded. His instincts rose from the base of his spine, telling him Sabra spoke the truth. "Motivated by your sense for fair play? Just because I believed you did not harm the palace guards does not mean—"

"Believe what you want." Aaron pulled a folded manila envelope from his pocket. "Or you can believe this."

Quamar took the envelope, opened it and pulled out an autopsy report. His eyes scanned the words.

"It was an airtight case against Trygg, Quamar."

"Trygg was tried for treason and the deaths of fifty military personnel," Quamar replied. "Emily McKnight was not mentioned in any of the files."

"Senator Keith Harper is Emily's father," Aaron explained. "He pulled some major strings to keep her death out of the public eye. And out of the military trial because her murder wouldn't have made a difference in the outcome. Trygg was sentenced to death based on the death of Booker's men. His execution date was set for less than a year away from now."

"Why didn't Senator Harper want her name included with the list of the victims?"

"Privacy. Emily was pregnant," Aaron said after a moment. "That part of Booker's file was true. Emily went to find Booker at the base the day of the deaths. She used her father's name to get through the security gates. The guards were green. Most of the victims were. Trygg didn't want any of his experienced military men killed."

"Of course not," Quamar said derisively.

"It appeared to be a series of mishaps," Aaron explained.

"Appeared to be?"

Aaron shrugged. "Let's just say that I don't believe in mishaps or coincidences when Trygg is involved."

Quamar grunted. "Go on."

"Booker had been called away at the last minute

to deal with another security matter off-site. Emily didn't know that, of course, and the guards failed to tell her. By the time anyone realized she'd breached security, Trygg had already pumped the area full of CIRCADIAN."

"I saw what the coroner reported." Quamar stared past Aaron's shoulder for a moment, processing. "She died sixteen hours later. First, she miscarried. After, the doctors could not stop the hemorrhaging."

"That part was true. The CIRCADIAN caused them both."

Silence filled the air between the men. Quamar studied Aaron for a moment, trying to figure out his motivation for sharing this information.

"Did you notice who the coroner was, Quamar?"

The giant glanced at the signature. His gaze darted back to Aaron. "Omar Haddad."

"A close personal friend of Senator Harper. And missing in action, as of three hours ago," Aaron stated, his tone grim.

"Omar has disappeared?"

"He and I were supposed to meet up earlier and approach you together," Aaron replied. "He never showed. Could be he's switched sides."

"His disappearance does not confirm Omar is guilty of conspiring with Trygg, Sabra—"

"I'm not done," Aaron interrupted, his voice hard. "Booker wasn't on base at the time of the poisoning, because he received last-minute orders. Orders to escort Omar Haddad back to Taer."

"For what reason?"

"A personal favor for General Trygg."

"What are you saying?"

"Trygg used Sandra to control her father."

"Booker knows of Sandra's involvement," Quamar stated. "If Omar thinks Booker would harm his daughter, he'd stop him."

"Booker knows. Somehow he got ahold of Trygg's file," Aaron admitted. "I haven't figured out how yet. It had been a closed military trial. No one except essential military personnel were allowed access. And all were ordered to remain silent."

"People talk, given the right persuasion. And files can be stolen," Quamar stated. "Booker had five years to do both."

"It took him less than two months." Aaron laughed with derision. "Booker found out almost immediately. He joined Labyrinth and headed over here within the first year after Emily's death."

"You and he could have had the same source. Who did you get your information from, Sabra?" Quamar demanded. "This kind of information just does not land at your feet."

Aaron's lips twisted into a wicked grin.

"I sold an airbus to a very important person in the United States government. An airplane that has a tracker located in its belly."

"How in the hell did you get ahold of an airplane?"

"It just so happens that I am a close personal friend of the President of the United States."

"The man who sent you to Leavenworth?" Quamar's laugh was low, guttural.

"What can I say?" Aaron shrugged. "I'm a forgiving person."

"And the favor you are asking? It is from the President?"

"Jon Mercer needs your help in wrapping up a very nasty situation that has been going on for many years. Are you up for it?"

Quamar snorted. "The President is your contact?"

Aaron shrugged. "Stranger things…"

"Why not go through Cain? Or come to me directly? Or Jarek for that matter?" Quamar frowned. "Why you?"

"Let's just say that this operation has been in the works for a while and that you, Cain and Jarek needed to be kept in the dark until the President decided otherwise."

"Too many people, too many complications." Quamar understood, but when it came to his loved ones… "I need proof, Sabra."

"Of course you do." Aaron reached into his pocket and pulled out a red scarf. "President Mercer also gave me a cool name. Cooler than the one he gave you, Cronus."

Cronus.

His Labyrinth code name. Quamar stiffened. Only a handful of people even knew of its existence. He hadn't heard the name in years. Not since he resigned from the organization.

"Mercer calls me…" Aaron draped the scarf over his face, wiggled his eyebrows. "Minos."

Chapter Sixteen

The cave lay deep on the west side of the cliffs, far above the ravine.

"Here," Sandra said, and wiped her fingers over the edge of the entrance. "My initials."

Booker noted that the *SH,* while worn from the weather, still remained.

Sandra took the flashlight from her bag, flipped the switch and pointed toward the back of the cave. "There should be a ledge at the top of the wall. I tucked the thermos in a crevice nearby."

"Let me." Booker stepped up. He took out his knife and dug between the stone and the hole. "It's wedged in tight."

He pulled out a plastic bag. Wrapped inside were several cylinders. Each not much bigger than a small silver thermos.

"Don't open it," she cautioned. "The nanites are pressurized inside. The serum will be active. Those cylinders, together, could wipe out half of a continent."

"So tell me again—" Booker placed the cylinders into the medical bag "—why you kept them?"

"I couldn't destroy them," she admitted, her voice suddenly weary. "I was so close, Booker. At the time, I couldn't let that go. Do you realize how hard it is to let something go that might help millions of people? If I could find the solution, the nanites could attack all different types of diseased cells. Including cancer cells. It would save millions of lives."

"Was it for that, or your father's approval?"

"I've asked the same question a million times," she acknowledged. She shoved her hair away from her face. "I think I grew up looking for some kind of recognition. From my father. From Jarek and Quamar. From the General."

"Why, Doc?" Booker asked, honestly puzzled. "You're smart. Beautiful." He thought of the families she helped. "Caring. Loving."

"My brother."

"Jamaal?"

Sandra couldn't hide the sadness. "No. Jamaal is the youngest. And irresponsible. He changes his profession as often as he changes clothes. It drives my father insane."

"I don't understand." Booker studied her face. Noticed the paleness of her cheeks.

"I had another, older brother. No one ever talks about him. Andon was born several years before the rest of us. He died when Jarek and Quamar were very small."

"How do you know about him?"

"My mother," Sandra answered. "She kept some of his things hidden from my father. I came home early one day and discovered her with them. She made me swear not to tell my father."

"How old were you?"

"Ten," she admitted. She leaned against the wall, hugged her arms to her chest.

"Andon had always been the one," Sandra explained. "My whole life I lived in the shadow of his ghost."

"At eleven, right before he died, he told my father he wished to be a surgeon," Sandra explained. "My father couldn't have been happier."

"Your mother told you that?"

"She broke down. One of the only times I've seen her that way."

"How did he die?"

"At the hands of the Al Asheera," Sandra replied. "They wanted my father to poison King Makrad, Jarek's father. When my father refused, they tied him up and made him watch while they killed his son.

"My father never recovered. I think that is why most of my life he kept a wall up between Jamaal and myself. He never allowed himself to love us fully."

"And so Jamaal reacted by being irresponsible."

"Yes. And he does it very well." Sandra laughed bitterly.

"And you followed in your father's footsteps.

You chose research to get his attention," Booker reasoned. "Was it the career you wanted?"

"Yes," she defended. "Even if I originally became a research scientist for my father, I learned to love my job."

"And the last few years? What about those?"

"I needed a break, Booker."

"No, Doc, you've been paying penance for screwing up. You came back here, stuck close to your father. Helping him with the royals, because of guilt."

"When I first found out about Andon, I used to daydream about how my family's life would have been so much better if he had lived. One big happy family."

Booker finally understood. "You pursued the research on rapid healing because of your brother's death."

"Yes," Sandra replied. "Logically, I couldn't have stopped his death, but somehow I'd always wished…"

"That you could have saved your brother." Booker sighed. "Nothing you do will bring Andon back."

"Maybe not," she acknowledged. "But with these cylinders, I might be able to save another family member."

Booker's eyes snapped to hers. "What do you mean?"

"I only told one person about my flight to Tourlay. The same person who told me Trygg had escaped."

"Who?"

"My father."

"YOU HAVE NO intention of destroying those cylinders, do you?" Booker demanded. "You need them for a bargaining chip with Trygg. You need to find out how deep your father is involved, and you think you can get Trygg to tell you if you promise him the cylinders."

"He's my father," she said simply.

"Damn it, Doc." Booker grabbed her arm, pulled her closer. "What makes you think Trygg will tell you the truth?"

"I have to try." She tugged on her arm, realized she wasn't going anywhere.

Sandra froze. She saw the anger. The icy blue eyes, the set of his jaw.

But he wasn't surprised.

"You knew, didn't you?" Sandra asked, her own rage making her words sharp. "You already knew my father was involved."

Booker paused a moment. That's when Sandra saw the flash of truth. If she hadn't been studying him so close she would've missed it.

"Don't you dare lie to me, McKnight." Her threat came out in a hiss.

"I suspected your father's involvement soon after I started my investigation five years ago," Booker acknowledged. "But if my suspicion is right, he's been involved much longer than that."

"Longer…" Sandra shook her head, sharp jerks

that showed her confusion, her fear and hurt. "Involvement in what?"

Booker noted the set of her chin, the stubborn line of her mouth, slamming it all back behind faith and trust in her father.

Brave. Loyal. Beautiful. Just like Aaron Sabra had said.

Booker stiffened. Damn it! He should have known. "Doc, does your father know Aaron Sabra?"

"No." She thought for a moment. "Not that I know of. Why?"

"Because Aaron told me about Trygg's escape only hours after it had happened. I don't like coincidences."

"Neither do I," Jim Rayo stated from the mouth of the cave entrance.

Sandra and Booker swung around. The colonel held a machine gun, its barrel leveled at Sandra.

"Hand me the bag, McKnight," he said almost pleasantly.

Two men stood behind him, both with matching machine guns. One keeping watch on the outside. The other staring at Sandra.

Booker stepped in front of Sandra. "You should listen to me when I tell you that you should walk away from all of this, Jim."

"I take orders from just one person, McKnight. Now if you move again, these bullets will go through you and into her," Rayo stated. "The only way you are going to keep her safe is to cooperate with me."

"How did you find us?" Sandra asked. "The storm washed out any tire tracks in the ravine."

Jim Rayo tapped the back of his head. "After my men kidnapped you, they inserted a GPS pin at the base of your skull. Under the skin."

Booker swore.

Sandra touched the base of her hairline, remembered the cut. "This whole chase was a setup?"

"You were always meant to get away," Jim explained. "McKnight managed to release you earlier than expected, but it all worked out."

He glanced at the bag. "We suspected you wouldn't give up their location easily, so we decided to let you lead us to the cylinders. Once I realized Booker came to the rescue, I sent men after you to throw off any suspicion and to motivate you to recover the cylinders. Then I tracked you here," Jim explained matter-of-factly.

Lewis Pitman stepped into the cave, his face flushed, his breath coming in short gasps. "You could've waited for me, Colonel."

"Hello, Lewis," Sandra spat. "You should have done us all a favor and fallen off the mountain."

"I missed you, too, Sandra," Lewis sneered, then turned to Jim. "Do you finally have them?"

"Give me the cylinders, McKnight," Jim ordered.

Slowly, Booker tossed the bag to Jim. The colonel caught it with his free hand. He glanced inside, then handed the bag off to Lewis. "Take this back to the helicopter."

"Helicopter?" Sandra frowned. "But I didn't hear—"

"They rappelled from above." Booker nodded toward the gear that hung from the colonel's waist.

"Always easier," Rayo answered, then caught Lewis before he left. "Have the men check the perimeter then join you. I'll be there in a few minutes. With our prisoners."

When Lewis hesitated, Jim snapped, "That's an order, Lewis."

Lewis frowned, but said nothing. Instead, he turned on his heel and walked out of the cave.

"He doesn't like you, Rayo," Booker commented, smirking. "Imagine that."

Jim's jaw tightened, but he remained silent, waited until Lewis left. "I have a few questions before we go, McKnight."

"I see you're still scraping and bowing to the general." Booker's gaze stayed on Rayo's weapon. "I figured you would have smartened up by now. Most of those who work for Trygg end up dead. Yet he still continues to thrive."

"Those who have died did so for the right reasons or because they betrayed those same reasons," Jim replied. "Trygg's vision is sound, Booker."

"Even if his mind isn't?"

"I don't want your opinions—I want answers," Jim snapped. "That day when your men died. At Osero. Why were you called away?"

"All right. Since you have the gun, I'll go along," Booker replied with a shrug. "I was ordered to escort Doctor Omar Haddad back to Taer. As his personal envoy."

Sandra gasped. "My father? You were with my father?"

"Yes." Booker's gaze caught and held hers, willing her to leave the questions until later.

"Who issued those orders?" Jim demanded.

"Trygg." Booker widened his stance. "Surprised me, too. So much, I verified the orders with Senator Harper."

Jim's fist tightened on the weapon. "That's impossible. Leaving you alive served no purpose. If anything, it placed the operation in jeopardy."

"I'm flattered that you think so much of me, Jim," Booker mocked. "Trygg's reasoning might not make sense to you, but then again, Trygg isn't known for sharing all aspects of his strategies. It's not his style. You know that better than anyone."

When Jim didn't answer, Booker took advantage of the silence and shifted forward. Jim lifted the machine gun to his shoulder. "I'm surprised, McKnight, not stupid. You take another step and I will kill you."

"Just wanted to hear you better." Booker raised

his hands, but his feet stayed planted. "Trygg played you from the beginning, Jim."

"That's a lie." Jim spoke low, clipped each word off with a razor-sharp edge.

"He undermined your self-confidence, taking advantage of the one mistake you made when you were twenty-two years old."

"He saved me from my mistake."

"He set you up."

Jim's eyes narrowed. "I've had it with your theories, McKnight—"

"I've had five years. That's a long time to learn about one's enemies," Booker reasoned. "And if you know anything about me, you know I'm thorough."

Jim waved his gun toward the cave entrance. "We're done here—"

"Did you know that the man you killed at the bar was there with a friend?"

"Yes," Jim said abruptly, his features slanted with the uncomfortable memory. "The friend testified against me. Gerald Ivers. He was the prosecution's main witness."

"All arranged by Trygg."

Jim snorted. "Trygg wasn't interested in me. Hell, at the time I'd only been in his outfit for a month."

"Don't fool yourself. Trygg requested you." Booker glanced back at Sandra. "Just like he did with the doc here. You'd only been military for a few short years, yet you were catching the eye of the upper brass."

"I was a damn kid," Jim argued, but doubt clouded his blue eyes.

Booker pressed his advantage. "Do you remember any of it? That night at the bar?"

"I remember all of it," he answered, his voice hollow now, his pain unconcealed.

"Gerald Ivers picked the fight. Got you so heated up, you drew your knife. When you swung at him, he caught your hand holding the knife, brought it down, sidestepped, then drove it into his buddy's stomach. With your help, of course. Then he testified later that you'd intentionally stabbed his friend."

"You're wrong," Jim snapped. "You weren't there."

"No, but one of the waitresses witnessed the attack," Booker explained. "She was too afraid to say anything to the authorities, but had no problem telling me. Especially after she heard about Gerald Ivers."

"What happened to Ivers?"

"He died a week after you were sent to prison."

"It doesn't matter. I stabbed Ivers's friend," Jim argued. "I was drunk. They were standing so close. I didn't realize the knife was in my hand until..."

"You were drugged," Booker stated. "Pretty much the same way you drugged Sergeant Tom Levi the night before you liberated Trygg from that military prison truck."

Jim stiffened. "How the hell did you know that?"

"It's typical Trygg style. Set the victim up with a friend. In Tom's case, it was Sergeant Harold Coffey. Then Trygg kills the friend, too."

"Coffey was a disgrace to the uniform. A low-life—"

"They usually are," Booker interrupted. "Gerald Ivers, a few weeks after he testified against you, ended up dead in the Potomac. He went swimming drunk one night and drowned."

"Ivers's death doesn't change the fact that I killed his friend." Jim shook his head. "I'd just lost my wife in a car accident. She'd taken a curve too quickly. I was grieving. Angry. Out of my mind."

"Jim," Booker said softly. "Your wife had a perfect driving record. She had driven that same route to work a thousand times. Why do you think, on that particular night, she took that curve too quickly?"

"She was a nurse. She'd worked a double shift—"

"How many times had she worked a double shift in her career? A hundred times? A thousand?"

Anger festered with the doubt. "You're lying. The coroner's report said it was accidental—no toxic substances were found in her blood—"

"Do you remember who performed the autopsy?"

He tried, but the memory was fuzzy. He'd read it at the bar, after he'd started drinking. "No."

"It was the same doctor who performed my wife's autopsy," Booker stated flatly. "And we both know Emily didn't die of a miscarriage."

LEWIS STEPPED UP ONTO the ridge and unclipped his harness, disgusted. Enough with the walk down memory lane.

Another reason Jim Rayo did not deserve the respect General Trygg bestowed on him.

Lewis had his own plans. And they didn't include General Trygg or Jim Rayo.

"You and you." He pointed at two of the men standing guard by the Black Hawk helicopter. "Help the colonel escort the prisoners when he's done with his conversation. I will have the pilot relocate down at the base of the ravine and meet you all there."

"Yes, sir." Lewis watched the two men disappear over the ledge, then climbed up into the helicopter.

"Let's go." Lewis slid on his radio earphones, then raised his hand and pointed down. "Take us to the ravine."

"Yes, sir." The pilot flipped the ignition switches and then hit the button to set the blades in motion.

A moment later, the radio beeped in Lewis's ear. "Pitman."

"Lewis, it's General Trygg. I need to speak with Colonel Rayo. He isn't answering my transmission."

"He isn't available, General." Lewis kept the satisfaction from his tone. Just.

"Have you obtained the cylinders?"

"Yes, sir. We have," Lewis answered. "But our flight back has been delayed."

"Delayed?" Trygg snapped. "What's the problem?"

"The colonel is interrogating McKnight and Doctor Haddad," Lewis responded. "I am to meet them at a pickup point down at the base of the ravine when he is done."

"Interrogating?"

"Yes, sir." Lewis leaned back in his seat, pictured the frown on Trygg's features. "The colonel was questioning McKnight regarding some information on a bar fight several years back."

"I see," General Trygg replied before pausing a long moment. "You have the cylinders in your possession, Lewis?"

"Yes, sir."

Another pause. "When they return to the helicopter, I want Doctor Haddad restrained. Then I want you to dispose of Booker McKnight. I don't want him found, Lewis. Understand me?"

"Colonel Rayo won't like—"

"That's an order, Doctor," Trygg snapped.

"Yes, sir," Lewis answered. "And if Colonel Rayo objects?"

"Tell him to report to me when you land," General Trygg said. "I'll take care of any objections."

The trip down to the base of the ravine took mere

minutes. Beyond the windshields lay an ocean of loose sand and rolling dunes. A good place to dump a body. Give the vultures a day, and no one would ever find McKnight.

After all, he had his orders. Lewis's lips twisted. But very few carried as much satisfaction.

"Let's go," Rayo yelled from the edge of the ravine, catching Lewis's attention.

The men prodded Booker and Sandra up into the helicopter. Lewis grabbed a set of handcuffs from a nearby bag, tossed them to the nearest guard. "Cuff her."

"What are the handcuffs for?" Jim demanded.

"General Trygg's direct orders, Colonel. He wants Doctor Haddad and McKnight restrained," Lewis sneered. He glanced at the man nearest the doctor. "Do it."

Sandra winced when the handcuffs clamped around her wrists.

"A waste of steel, right, Rayo?" Booker's eyes narrowed as the guards handcuffed his wrists in front of him. "I won't be finishing this ride, will I?"

Jim looked at Lewis, who shrugged and turned back in his seat. "Take it up with the general, Colonel."

The pilot pulled back on the throttle.

The floor jolted under Sandra's feet, tossing her off balance. She grabbed for the nearest beam with both hands.

Suddenly, bullets ripped across the windshield, over the outside of the helicopter.

"Hold on!" the pilot yelled, then jerked the throttle, banked the helicopter around.

Equipment flew against the walls, through the open door. Men scrambled against the tilt, slammed into the back of the helicopter.

Booker shifted, catching himself on a hanging strap, his eyes on Lewis.

Lewis grabbed the wall, raised his pistol.

"No!" Sandra gripped the beam harder, swung her legs up and kicked Booker square in the back.

"Grab McKnight!" Rayo yelled. But the warning came too late.

Booker flew through the open doorway and dropped two stories to the desert below.

"Make sure she doesn't cause more trouble!" Lewis ordered.

Sandra spun around saw the pistol gripped in one of the guards' meaty fists.

Pain exploded in her temple and then she fell.

Into a deep, black void.

BOOKER BLINKED, FORCING his eyes to open against the glare of the sun, the sharp stabs of pain as his body woke.

She shoved him out of the helicopter!

Booker focused, spit out the grains of sand, then

raised himself up on his hands. When he got ahold of the doc's beautiful neck, he'd wring it.

He took a quick inventory of his injuries. Sprained wrist, twisted shoulder. When he shifted to his knees, pain jabbed his side.

Bruised ribs.

"Well, well." The voice drifted over him, prodded him between his shoulder blades with the barrel of a machine gun. "That was quite a free fall you took, McKnight."

"I told you he survived, Boba."

Booker turned over, took in the Contee brothers standing a few feet away. "You were the ones who fired on the helicopter, weren't you?"

"Guilty." Madu Contee smiled lopsidedly through a fat bottom lip, revealing a fresh gap in his teeth. "Although, we were just trying to damage it enough to force a landing."

"We stopped when we saw you falling," Boba added. "We weren't allowed to shoot you."

"That was orders. This isn't." Without warning, Madu kicked him, catching him in the stomach.

Pain ripped through Booker's gut. He rolled over, sucking in oxygen.

"*That* was for wiping out all my merchandise at the warehouse, McKnight." He dragged Booker up by the collar, putting them almost nose to nose. "A half million dollars of weapons…gone."

"And a few of your teeth it seems."

"More than that," Boba commented, his brow creased, his tone serious. "The office chair shot back and hit him in the crotch—"

"Shut up, Boba," Madu warned. He dropped Booker and advanced on his brother, his fists tight.

"What did I say?" Boba put his hands up, confused. "You screamed loud. I heard you over the ringing in my ears—"

"Damn it, Boba!" Madu slapped his brother upside his head. "You just never know when to stop talking—"

"I don't have time for family squabbles, boys." Booker maneuvered himself to his knees, then stood. "Either kill me or take me to Minos."

TAER'S HOSPITAL AND MEDICAL offices occupied one of the city's tallest buildings. Twenty-four floors to be exact.

Although Doctor Omar Haddad had worked on all twenty-four floors at one time or another, the basement was where he preferred. Where he found his solitude.

Alone with his thoughts, his equipment and the dead for company.

The vault was what most of those who worked with him called the coronor's lab.

A long, wide room of tiled white flooring and concrete walls covered half the length of the hospital wing. Its farthest wall was little more than a bank of mortuary refrigerators, large enough to house fifty bodies.

Omar Haddad stood in the middle of the room, amidst the ten examining tables, all of which were empty except one.

He stared down at the man on the table. Senator Keith Harper. Once a friend, a colleague—who turned on his country at the whim of his daughter and her greed.

Senator Harper, a man in need of the love of his daughter. Until her need for money destroyed her, and in its aftermath, him, too.

The other man groaned, and his eyes blinked open, clearing the haze of the drug away.

"What the hell?" Harper focused on Omar. He struggled to rise. For the first time Omar saw fear and panic in his friend's features.

"You told the wrong person that you were coming after me." Omar reached over to his surgical tray and grabbed surgical gloves. With deft fingers, he snapped the gloves over his hands. "Minos owed me a favor. He told me you were on your way. You are a creature of habit, my friend. Something you learn not to be when you work as a spy. It took very little effort to arrange for your hotel water to be drugged."

Harper looked down the length of the table, realized he'd been strapped in across the chest, arms and legs. Still, he struggled against the bindings.

"Save your strength for what's coming. You're

going to need it," Omar ordered. "You aren't going anywhere, Keith. Not until you tell me what I want to know."

"You killed my daughter," Keith spat out. "What makes you think I'll help you?"

"Trygg killed your daughter before I could stop him," Omar corrected. "I should have never told you the truth behind her death. If I'd let you believe she died by accident—"

"But you didn't," Harper sneered. "And now you know how it feels to lose a child to Trygg."

"I've already lost a child, Keith. Years before I even knew you. I watched my little boy, Andon, die in front of my eyes, because I refused to kill a good friend of mine." Omar picked up a thin scalpel. "I won't make that mistake again. Sandra will not pay the price for the choices I've made in my past, like so many others in my family."

"If you know Minos, you have the coordinates to Trygg's camp."

"He's moved his airbus."

"Which means he has your daughter," Keith taunted. "I'm not going to help you save her, you son of a bitch."

"Oh, I think you will. Pain is a great motivator, Keith."

"I'll die first."

Omar's face hardened. "No. You'll just wish you had."

THE TENT WAS RED. Bloodred. A beacon amidst the bland brown of the sand it sat upon.

Arrogant.

They'd traveled by jeep. Over two hours of listening to the brothers' bickering. And when that got old, they enumerated the virtues of their new leader, Minos.

Once they got to camp—a camp surprisingly clean, with families crowding the sand, watching—hundreds of eyes stared at the men from over red scarves.

"One big happy family," Booker murmured, then stretched the cramps out of his shoulders and arms. He slipped the shim back into his wristwatch, then strained against the unlocked handcuffs, applying just enough pressure so as not to raise the brothers' suspicions.

"My family," Madu snapped, and raised his rifle butt. Pain exploded between Booker's shoulder blades. He fell to his hands and knees, then gripped the sand, held the grains in his fist until the pain eased.

"Get up." Boba grabbed him by the arm, dragged him to his feet. "The boss is done waiting."

He shoved Booker through one of tents at the edge of the encampment.

"McKnight."

Booker jerked around to the sound of laughter. His hands tightened around the sand still in his fist.

Black eyes crinkled at the corners, the only feature visible over the red scarf.

"Minos." Booker's spine went rigid. "I'm glad I amuse you."

The Al Asheera leader glanced from Booker to the brothers then back again. "I have to say when Madu called his find in, I was a little surprised. I didn't expect you'd be so easy."

"He'd been thrown out of a flying helicopter," Boba responded, smirking. "Knocked him stupid."

"How did you know how to find the helicopter?" Booker asked.

Minos shook his head. "First my questions."

Booker glanced around the tent, noted the bar, the leather recliner, the pillows and curtains and bed in the corner. "Terrorism seems to pay well these days."

"Yes, it does," Minos replied evenly. He pulled out a 9mm Glock from his robes, pointed it at Booker's chest.

"I need to have a talk with our friend here, gentlemen." Minos's gaze locked with Madu's. "Run that errand for me. The one we discussed earlier."

Booker watched the brothers leave. "So now that we are alone…" He turned back toward the other man. "You can lose the scarf, Sabra."

Aaron laughed, then tugged the cloth from his face. The gun stayed on Booker. "Quamar said you were smarter than you looked."

"You're sure he didn't say I was smarter than you?" Booker took a step closer, tightened his fist.

"He might have, but don't let it go to your head."

Without warning, Booker dropped the cuffs off his wrists, then heaved the sand at Aaron's face.

Aaron swore, lowered the gun, grasped his eyes.

Booker grabbed the other man's gun and slammed his fist into his jaw.

Aaron hit the floor, stunned. He lay there for a few seconds, blood flowing from his lip. "Damn it. I should have seen that coming."

Before he could move, Booker shoved the pistol under the other man's jaw and jammed it up until his head locked back. "I should kill you right now."

"First tell me how you figured it out."

"It wasn't hard. The fact that you knew about Sandra's flight out of Taer. And how much you care for the Al Asheera." He nodded toward the chair. "The first recliner I've seen in a tent."

"Picked up on that, did you?"

"I also picked up on the red tent. I bet it went a long way in establishing your authority with the Al Asheera. You thumbed your nose at discovery from your enemies. Defied anyone to stop you. Most would have been worried about satellites spotting your location. But Taer doesn't own satellites and the United States—the only other country that would be interested in your activities—already knew of your location. In fact, they approved. Or should I say, the President approved."

"Impressive, McKnight."

"You've yet to see impressive." Booker shoved the gun barrel a little harder. "I want to know how you found me and where Trygg took Sandra. Or a bullet will go through your head and the floor will match your tent."

"WAKE UP, DOCTOR HADDAD."

Sandra heard the voice, felt the thumb and finger clamp down on her chin.

She opened her eyes, forced them to focus.

Trygg smiled at her, leaned in and gave her a soft kiss on her lips.

Sandra tried to shove him away, but didn't have any feeling in her arms. She looked up, saw the handcuffs looped through the chain. Bile slapped at the back of her throat.

"I see you remember being in this exact situation in Taer a few days ago."

"You ordered me to be restrained this way." The words came out in a dull disbelief.

"I guess I'm not the father figure type, after all." Trygg stepped back and laughed. A dry, wicked laugh that left Sandra's insides tight, nauseated.

"You disgust me."

"Lucky me," Trygg added. "Otherwise I might

have found myself flying out of a helicopter. Isn't that what you did to your last lover?"

"McKnight isn't my lover, General. My reaction was instinctive," Sandra lied. Hoping to distance herself from Booker. "Pitman was going to shoot McKnight at point-blank range. On your orders."

"So you saved him, by kicking him out of a helicopter going forty miles an hour and a hundred feet in the air?"

"I don't like the sight of blood," she quipped. This man deserved no more of her fear, only her contempt. "Except maybe yours."

"Not very doctorlike, Sandra." Trygg's own anger surfaced.

"We both know what kind of doctor I am," Sandra observed. "And what kind of man you are."

"And yet…" He pointed through the tent window. "We are on the precipice of *my* success."

The airplane sat in the flats of the Sahara. A makeshift runway, a long snake of asphalt, lay in its path. The white hull gleamed in the sun, its netting now piled in a mound nearby.

No camouflage meant Trygg was no longer hiding. "I won't help you kill innocent people," Sandra insisted.

"Jim Rayo gave Lewis Pitman the cylinders," Trygg replied. "And the doctor has had five years to study up on CIRCADIAN."

"It would take him five lifetimes to understand my equations," Sandra scoffed.

"He barely has one lifetime, actually," Trygg responded dryly.

She understood then. "You're going to kill Lewis, too, aren't you?"

"Like I said, I have the cylinders. And there are many greedy research doctors in the world."

Instinctively, she pulled against the handcuffs, strained away from the pole.

"You're hurting yourself for no reason."

Harsh red rivulets trailed down her arms. The pain was minimal, her arms numb.

"I thought you were smarter than that." Trygg grabbed her arm, smeared the blood with his thumb. "How would the nanites react to your organs, Doctor Haddad?"

Sandra jerked her arm away. "I'm smart enough to know you won't get away with this, Trygg. Booker will stop you—"

"Not before I kill your family and your friends." The glint in his eye, the insanity of it, made her sick with fear. "You see, I don't fear death, Doctor Haddad. I've been at war long enough to understand that I might end up a casualty."

"This isn't about the serum, is it?"

Trygg put his thumb and finger together, leaving a small space between. "It is a little bit."

"This is about me. And revenge."

"You betrayed me." The evil filled his features, slanted them into ugly fury before sliding into a wicked smile. "You and your father. I cannot let that go unpunished."

"My father?"

"Your father was my associate. He arranged for you to work with me on the project. He helped Senator Harper obtain the supplies and equipment for Lewis Pitman."

"No, he would not have—"

"You have no idea what your father is capable of," Trygg mused. "Right now, I find it more satisfying not to enlighten you. Maybe later."

"I'll make sure you never live that long," Sandra promised through tight teeth. "So help me, God."

"You forget, I pretty much am God," Trygg reminded her. "You and Booker McKnight will never change that fact."

"I don't need him to stop you."

"Brave words," Trygg mused. "Of course, Mc-Knight could have died falling out of that helicopter. So you might be on your own. Not something you're unfamiliar with, correct, Sandra?"

"He'll be here." The jab hit deep, like it was meant to. "It would take more than that…or you…to kill him."

"I hope so, Doctor Haddad." Trygg's smile cut across his face in a vicious twist. He took out his knife and grabbed her hair. "I hope it takes the whole Sahara Desert."

"What do you mean?" She pulled away until he tightened her hold, made her cry out.

"I think it's time to play a little hide-and-seek with your boyfriend." He jerked her head forward, then dug the tip of his knife in at the base of her scalp.

Sandra bit her lip, refusing to cry out at the hot, searing pain.

"This tracking device will help." Trygg held up the bloody microchip. "You might be surprised to learn that I found a similar tracking device in my plane. Of course, I left it at my old camp."

Trygg's gaze narrowed on hers. "I don't suppose you know who planted it there, do you?"

"Pitman," Sandra lied. "He wants the glory. I'm guessing he made a deal with the Al Asheera."

Trygg's mouth twisted into a vicious grin. "Clever, Doctor Haddad. But you and I both know Lewis doesn't have the courage or intelligence to take me on." He placed the microchip in his pocket. "It doesn't matter. Right now, I'm jamming both signals."

"Booker will come, Trygg."

"But will he find you or the plane?" He tipped her chin, his gaze locked with hers. "My bet's on you."

"I WANT TO know how you found us, Sabra." Booker stepped back and motioned with the pistol for Aaron to stand.

"So you can go after Sandra half-cocked and get yourself killed?" Aaron rubbed his jaw and got to his feet. "I don't think so. I've got a lot of money tied up in your survival, McKnight."

"What the hell are you talking about?"

"Read this." Aaron grabbed a file from the bar and tossed it at Booker's feet. "Then decide if you want to do this on your own."

Booker dropped to the papers to the ground. "Why should I trust you?"

"Because it holds the truth." Quamar stepped through the opening in the tent. "I have read the file."

"What the hell are you doing here?" Aaron demanded. "You were supposed to find Sandra's father."

"Omar Haddad is nowhere in the city," Quamar answered, his tone matching Aaron's. "He has gone rogue."

"Why don't you both enlighten me, Sabra?" Booker held the gun steady. "And we'll move this meeting right along."

"Let us treat this as a civilized meeting." Quamar walked over to his friend and placed his hand on the gun.

"I love Sandra as I would a sister. You are not the only one who is afraid for her safety, Booker. But you need to hear everything," Quamar stated. "Then you can react with anger."

Booker forced his body to relax. He lowered the gun. "I'm listening."

"About thirty years ago, Omar Haddad inadvertently started the chain of events we're dealing with today." Aaron walked over to the bar, poured himself two fingers of whiskey, then turned back. "With one bad decision. A decision he based on the death of his eldest son, Andon."

"The doc told me about her brother. How the Al Asheera forced Omar to watch while they killed him."

"She told you that?" Quamar asked, surprised.

"Yes. She found out when she was ten. Why?"

"She never told me or Jarek or anyone else, for that matter," Quamar responded. "I find that interesting, considering she does not like you, Booker."

Aaron snorted, but made no comment. "Andon Haddad's death started a series of events that included the death of Jarek's parents and Quamar's mother."

"And now Sandra's life is in jeopardy." Booker glanced at the giant. "How long have you known?"

"I read the file several hours ago," Quamar answered. "But it makes no difference. Omar is not my enemy. The Al Asheera killed my mother. No one else was responsible."

"Explain that to Omar." Aaron downed the whiskey in one gulp. "Omar hired Trygg over thirty years ago to kill the head of the Al Asheera. The man responsible for Andon's death. In return, he promised Trygg government secrets. Trygg agreed and killed the man."

"Unfortunately, my youngest uncle, Hassan, wanted Taer's crown. He secretly stepped in as the new Al Asheera leader," Quamar explained. "Once Hassan established himself as the leader, over the next several years, he arranged for the murder of Jarek's parents. And many others loyal to the crown."

"Omar blames himself for their deaths," Aaron explained.

"And the government secrets Trygg gained from Omar?" Booker asked, but he already knew the answer. "What were they?"

"Everything the United States had on rapid healing serums."

"Super Soldiers," Booker commented, understanding. "Omar introduced Trygg to the concept."

"Exactly," Aaron replied. "Which only adds your men to the list Omar feels he is responsible for."

"At some point, after my mother, Theresa Bazan's, death, Omar came clean to Jon Mercer." Quamar crossed his arms. "Jon was the Director of Labyrinth at the time. He convinced Omar to become a double agent."

"But Trygg turned out to be a slippery bastard," Aaron added. "Mercer couldn't get anything on him—not without implicating Omar—until Trygg got himself placed on the research committee for CIRCADIAN several years ago. By then Trygg had maneuvered himself into a four-star general position and accumulated enough money for leverage to get what he wanted."

"And Sandra? Why would Omar agree to her assignment to the research?"

"When Trygg heard about Sandra's research, he called Omar and threatened him. Omar called Mercer. Mercer convinced Omar that Sandra's research could bring down Trygg. Omar had no choice. Not after Jon managed to keep Omar's involvement under wraps. Mercer promised Sandra safety from Trygg by placing Kate MacAlister-D'Amato in charge of the research. At the time, Mercer had considered bringing her on board with Labyrinth."

"But Kate didn't stay assigned long enough to even be briefed on the situation," Booker guessed. "Trygg wanted her removed almost immediately."

"To make matters worse, Omar helped Trygg cover up the death of Jim Rayo's wife several years before."

"It was part of the original deal," Quamar added. "Omar would offer his medical services, off the radar, for Trygg whenever he needed them."

"Trygg contacted Omar and hinted at the possibility he might need him to sign another death certificate."

"Kate's," Booker guessed.

"Right," Aaron answered. "Mercer had Kate re-assigned. And protected. Trygg brought in Lewis Pitman."

"And eventually Sandra turned on Trygg," Booker concluded, understanding.

"Yes," Aaron responded. "Once Trygg went to prison, Mercer found me at Leavenworth. I was to get on Trygg's good side, join his ranks. It took me a long time, a couple months, but I managed to earn Trygg's trust. Then one day I got jumped in the yard by a stoned-out psychopath with a homemade knife. I spent six months in the infirmary recovering. My opportunity was lost. Trygg didn't want anything to do with me afterward."

"So Mercer sprung you and set you up as the Al Asheera leader?" Booker asked the question.

Aaron shrugged. "Wasn't hard. A few years ago, King Jarek destroyed the tribe, brought down the last leader, a woman, who was trying to take over Taer's new oil supply. Jon Mercer arranged for me to have money. From a private source. The Al Asheera were near poverty, in hiding and desperate for help."

"Private source?"

"It doesn't matter," Aaron explained. "With the money, Mercer helped me get government equipment to Trygg—equipment Keith Harper couldn't get his hands on without putting him under suspicion."

"Aaron has been working with Senator Harper

and Colonel Rayo for over the past year," Quamar added. "As Minos."

"How is this history going to save Sandra now?"

"I received the frequency codes to the tracking device Rayo's men planted on Sandra."

"Madu and Boba found us at the helicopter through the doc's tracking device," Booker acknowledged.

"Madu would've been there earlier, but the storm slowed them up. Also, we didn't have access to a helicopter. Trygg does."

"Where did you get the frequency code?"

"I found Senator Harper, dead, in Omar's private office." Quamar sighed, then placed his hands on his hips. "And he did not die quickly. Omar tortured him."

"Harper went there to kill Omar. The man had no combat skill, easy pickings for someone with Omar's experience," Aaron inserted. "He got the frequency code for Sandra's tracking chip. Left it with Keith Harper's body."

"Did Harper know that Trygg captured Sandra in the cave? That he has the cylinders?" Booker asked.

"No," Aaron said after a moment. "Harper had a meeting scheduled with Omar last night. I warned Omar that Harper might try to kill him. And that Harper had the frequency codes. He'd given me the one to Trygg's camp. But the frequency has been jammed. And the camp has been moved. The men I left to watch were discovered and killed."

"Why didn't you just kill Trygg when you had the chance?" Booker demanded. "You've been dealing with him since his escape."

"I was under orders from President Mercer. I wasn't allowed to take him into custody until I had evidence that the cylinders were contained and not left somewhere to detonate," Aaron answered. "I wasn't about to let my people get caught up in this mess, either."

"Your people."

"You have a problem with that statement?" Aaron demanded. "Because they are the same people your girlfriend cares for."

Booker grunted, but let the comment pass. "So this has nothing to do with the oil site. There is a lot of oil under that ground. If Taer is destroyed, that ground and everything around it might become contaminated. That means a lot of money to the United States."

"It does," Aaron agreed. "While it might be Mercer's motivation, it is not mine."

"Last question," Booker said and raised the pistol, once more pointing at Aaron. "Who told Trygg that Sandra was leaving for Tourlay?"

Aaron put his hands high in the air. "So you can shoot the messenger?"

Booker thumbed the hammer back on the pistol.

"All right, damn it. I did," Aaron confessed. "Under orders."

"From who?"

"President Mercer. It secured my place in Trygg's plans." Aaron stared straight down the barrel. "But in the spirit of full disclosure, Mercer ordered me to protect her. And with her help, recover the cylinders before Trygg. I just figured you would do a better job."

"That doesn't sound like you," Quamar observed wryly.

"Unless…" Quamar took a long, curious look at Booker. The brown eyes softened, thoughtful. "I understand."

"Understand what?" Booker demanded.

"You are in love with Sandra," Quamar stated.

Aaron grinned. "Just call me Cupid."

"You son of a bitch," Booker bit out, and took a step forward.

"Boss," Madu yelled, and rushed into the tent. He stopped dead in his tracks; his eyes ran up and down Aaron. "You?" The smuggler glanced from one man to the next, taking in the situation. "You are Minos."

Aaron ignored the surprise. "What do you have, Madu?"

"We picked up the signal on Doctor Haddad's chip. The jamming disengaged about three minutes ago. We also picked up the frequency on the airbus.

Both are in opposite directions and at least a dozen hours from here by vehicle."

Quamar stepped in front of Booker's gun. "Well, it is a good thing that I chose to come here by helicopter."

"GENERAL?" JIM RAYO stormed into the tent. "Doctor Pitman has informed me that Sandra Haddad has been moved to an undisclosed location."

The general set down his pen on the desk, took off his glasses and leaned back in his chair.

"Yes. That was my order. Sandra Haddad is fine, for the time being." He studied the colonel for a second or two. "How is Doctor Pitman coming along with his lab?"

"He just informed me that he needs another six to eight hours to get the cylinders ready for disbursement."

"Good." Trygg paused a moment, frowning. "And the tracking chip for the plane?"

"A hundred miles away, dropped somewhere over the desert as ordered, sir."

"Thank you, Jim." Trygg sat back in his chair. "How long have we worked together, Jim?"

"Twenty-five years, sir."

"Twenty-five years," Trygg repeated, then sighed. "It never seems as long as it sounds."

"Yes, sir."

"Are you proud of your life? Are you proud of

your career, and what we've accomplished over all these years?"

"Yes, sir."

"I'm not so sure." Trygg studied the man before him. "You're a good man, Colonel Rayo. The best soldier I've known. And I've known many."

"Likewise, sir. I've always trusted your judgment. I've followed your orders for the past thirty years, General."

"And you have concerns with this mission—am I correct?"

Jim gave him a sharp, affirmative nod. "Taer holds well over fifty thousand people."

The general placed his elbows on the armrests. Linked his fingers in front of him. "Not all will die, Jim. We have only two cylinders to drop."

"Half will die," Jim answered, his stance widening. "We have no idea of the effect on others. There are women and children who will be killed, General."

"So you do have a problem with my decision," Trygg observed. "This isn't the first time we've dealt with collateral damage."

"In the past, all collateral damage were military men. Recruits. Their families received honorable compensations," Jim argued.

"So after all these years, you're questioning my judgment. Right at the precipice of our biggest triumph."

"Sir, we'll lose civilian—"

"We've lost civilians before, damn it!" Anger flashed deep in Trygg's eyes, maybe a hint of insanity.

Jim ignored both. He saw nothing but the image of his wife, her broken body. "My wife was one of those civilians, wasn't she, General?"

Trygg's gaze snapped to Jim's. In that moment, Jim understood that everything Booker had told him about the bar fight and his wife had been true.

"I had nothing to do with your wife's death, Jim."

"And Emily McKnight's? Or her unborn child's?"

"We've been over this before, Jim. Emily and her child were unknown factors in an otherwise sound equation. Her death wasn't preventable," Trygg explained. "You understand every mission does not go smoothly. It's expected. She was unexpected."

"I don't believe she was, General. I believe you brought her into the equation on purpose."

Trygg laughed and shook his head. "Like I said, we've known each other too long, haven't we?"

"I'm beginning to think I don't know you at all, sir."

"You're right, Jim." Trygg spread his hands in a helpless gesture. "I did allow Emily McKnight access through the gates. But it was necessary. She had too much control over her father. It had become a problem when she broke through the gates."

"So you killed his daughter," Jim stated. It was no longer a question to him, but a fact.

"It was necessary."

Trygg slid open the drawer of his desk.

Jim caught the look. The one that had been growing in the back of the general's eyes since the rescue. A madness.

Jim grabbed his gun, pointed it at the general. "Keep your hands where I can see them, sir."

"I was reaching for a cigar."

"You killed my wife." Jim kept his hand level, his eyes pinned on the general. "Why?"

"All right. We do this your way." Trygg sighed, let his hands drop onto the desk, palms spread. "Your wife would have held you back from greatness. I needed you more than she did."

"You son of a bitch." Jim's finger tightened on the trigger. Suddenly, a gun fired from behind him. Pain exploded in Jim's back, took him to his knees. His stomach burned. Jim pulled his hand away, saw the blood coating his fingers.

Lewis stepped around him.

"Meet your replacement, Jim."

Lewis kicked Jim's gun across the tent.

"I told the general here about your conversation with McKnight, Colonel," Lewis explained. "From the moment he talked about your wife, you changed sides. Damnedest thing I've ever seen."

Jim tried to get his feet under him, but the strength wasn't there. "Sandra Haddad. Where is she?"

"At the runway," Lewis taunted. "We'll be taking care of her real soon."

"You won't get away with…" Jim drew a haggard breath. His back burned, but his legs and arms moved.

"With this? But I already have, Jim. I have to finish great tasks. While all you have left to do is die." Trygg stood behind his desk, pulled a gun out of his desk drawer and placed it in a side holster beneath his jacket. "Try to do it quickly."

Jim slumped to the floor in a pool of his own blood. He dragged in desperate breaths, breaching the pain that raged in his chest.

"It's time to take care of Doctor Haddad." Trygg stepped over him, then paused. "Give your wife my regards when you see her."

IT HAD TAKEN THEM three hours to reach the tracking device. Three hours the body lay in the sand. Vultures circling, until the roar of the helicopter chased them away.

"Just for the record, I am not comfortable out in the open like this, McKnight."

Booker jumped from the helicopter. He noted the body had been dumped on the low ground. "Doesn't matter."

"Does to me," Aaron muttered, then followed Booker a few yards to the body, his rifle raised. His eyes were on the dunes around them.

"It's not Sandra." Booker flipped over the body.

Instantly recognized the sand-covered features. "It's Jim Rayo."

"Hell." Aaron squatted next to Booker, examined the extent of the wound, the dried blood. "He's been dead for a few hours. Maybe half a day."

Booker grunted. "He was shot in the back. The bullet exited above the abdomen. But he didn't die right away. They dragged him out here and let him suffer a bit."

"My bet is that they shot him at their camp," Aaron said. "Which means we're close."

"Close means nothing in the Sahara." Booker let the body roll back, angry over the kind of man Rayo could have been if Trygg hadn't interfered with his life.

"Our position is risky at best." Aaron scanned the perimeter, stopped twice on their helicopter. "Too many dunes around us. We're sitting ducks down here."

Booker patted down Jim's shirt pocket. "I've got something." He pulled out the small microchip. "There's blood on it."

"Sandra's. Which means she could be alive," Aaron reasoned. He did a quick check of the pants pockets, then stopped. "Hold on."

Aaron grabbed Jim Rayo's left arm. "I'll be damned."

"That goes without saying," Booker quipped, then followed Aaron's gaze to Jim's outstretched hand.

Aaron turned the left cuff inside out. Booker recognized the numbers written in blood. "They're geographic coordinates. Rayo must have written them down before he died."

"In his own blood."

Bullets ripped across the hull of the helicopter, striking the windows. Pinned them down with nothing but the body for cover.

"Trygg's men." Aaron squinted at the horizon, trying to find the snipers. "Damn it, I knew this was a trap."

Another wave of gunfire ripped through the tail of the copter. All it took was one round to hit the gas tank, and the bird exploded, sending balls of fire and metal shards through the air.

"Quamar is not going to like that." Aaron swore and raised his rifle. "He's going to kill you."

"From the looks of things, he'll have to take his turn in line." Booker raised his rifle, fired at a distant movement among the bushes. A cry echoed across the sand. "There's too many, and they have the high ground."

Aaron took down another sniper and fired shots at two more who were quick enough to duck behind some boulders.

Suddenly, bullets ripped up the ground above them. The mercenaries scattered, screaming as their ranks broke under the barrage of gunfire.

"What the hell—" Military gunships rose over

the dunes, opening fire on the rest of Trygg's men. Within moments, the gun battle ceased.

Aaron swore. "Who—"

"Wait." Booker raised his rifle. Two helicopters settled on the ground a few yards away. "They might not be friendly."

Cain MacAlister, dressed in full desert military fatigues, jumped from the nearest helicopter. A moment later, Jarek Al Asadi followed, wearing identical fatigues.

"I'll be damned." When Booker stood, Aaron joined him. Three additional helicopters approached from the farthest ridge and landed by the others.

Military personnel—both Taer and U.S.—poured from the birds.

"Secure the area," Cain shouted to the nearest men. "Then watch the ridge in case more show."

Half the soldiers climbed the dunes; the others stayed to guard the helicopters and the King of Taer.

"How in the hell did you know where we were?" Aaron asked.

"Omar Haddad called the President," Cain admitted. "He informed Jon that Keith Harper was no longer a threat to national security. Then he gave him the frequency on the microchip. Omar led us to believe we were tracking the airbus."

"Omar wanted you to save his daughter," Booker stated, understanding. If Omar had the frequency to the airbus, he'd want to stop Trygg himself.

"We found Senator Harper, dead, in Omar's medical offices," Jarek explained. "Cain and Kate arrived in Taer earlier today. When Jon called Cain with the microchip frequency, I offered my assistance."

"I believe, Your Majesty, the exact words were, 'Either I help you, or you rot in my dungeons,'" Cain remarked.

"Quamar took my men," Aaron stated. "He's following the original frequency, possibly into a trap. We need to bring them back."

"Your men?" Jarek demanded. "Who are your men?"

"He's Minos," Booker stated. "Your new Al Asheera leader."

Aaron ignored Jarek's surprise, then anger. "The Al Asheera are heading to the southwest area of the Sahara. We need to warn them."

"Quamar is with the Al Asheera?" Jarek looked at Booker. "You approved of this plan?"

Booker shrugged, enjoying Jarek's bewilderment. "Not until the Contee brothers offered to act as Quamar's second lieutenants."

"What—"

"Let's go," Cain insisted. "We can radio Quamar, turn him back, then head to the correct coordinates. Booker and Aaron can give us a situation report on the way."

"This is Colonel Jim Rayo." Booker nudged the body with his toe. "Trygg's first in command. He left us geographic coordinates. That's where we'll find Trygg and Sandra."

"How can you be sure it's not another trap?"

"I know Trygg," Booker explained. "He sent us on a wild-goose chase. Then laid a trap. But the man is arrogant. He thinks he outmaneuvered us. And we've been taken out of the equation. If so, he'll leave himself vulnerable, just because he thinks he's indestructible now."

"You hope," Jarek added.

"Didn't I just say that?" Booker smirked. "No other alternative has presented itself."

"Then you sold me." Cain turned to one of his men. "Get on the radio." He nodded toward Aaron. "He'll give you the frequency and the camp coordinates. Inform Quamar Al Asadi that they need to head back. Tell him where."

Chapter Seventeen

"They're there," Cain observed, then adjusted his scope. The dunes sloped and rose under the moon and stars in waves of shadows. "Thermal imaging shows maybe fifty men."

Booker followed Cain's line of vision, noting Trygg's men were moving to the eastern outer boundary of the camp. "It looks like they're taking up positions to protect the airplane."

Cain's satellite phone buzzed. He grabbed it from his belt and punched a button. "MacAlister."

A moment later he checked his watch. "Got it."

"Quamar is an hour out with the Al Asheera, Jarek," Cain said, putting away the phone.

"So," Jarek acknowledged. "We wait."

"You wait," Booker stated. He checked his pistol, holstered it, then shoved additional clips into his pocket. "I'm going in to find Sandra."

"We're going to stop him, Booker." Jarek gripped his arm, stopping his friend. "And find Sandra, too. But the fact remains that Trygg plans on releasing

CIRCADIAN on my city. That's fifty thousand people. We can't risk tipping our hand too soon."

"You and I both know he'll kill her first," Booker stated, then yanked his arm free. He grabbed his rifle from the helicopter. "I'm going in, and I'm bringing her out."

"Hell," Aaron bit out. "I don't get my payoff unless Doctor Haddad walks away from this relatively healthy."

Aaron lifted his machine gun, checked the clips. "I'll go with him."

Jarek nodded. "You have an hour to get her out of there. By that time, Quamar is going to be here. And we are going to flatten that camp and everyone in it."

BOOKER SCANNED THE PERIMETER, his gun raised, his stance ready. He studied the airbus less than a hundred yards away. "But I don't like it."

Aaron took a step away from the nearest tent, then froze. "Booker, look at the netting by the plane."

Two guards lay unmoving, tangled in the web of rope.

"Omar," Booker bit out.

Omar Haddad, dressed in full military gear, stepped over another body and made his way to the steps into the airplane.

"Looks like Senator Harper gave him more than

the frequencies for the microchips." Aaron pulled out his binoculars, thumbed them into focus. "He must have given Omar the new camp location."

"Tent," Booker commented, annoyed. "Another dead soldier."

"Doesn't he know he's too old for this?" Aaron whistled, his eyes still on Omar. "Hell, we're too old for this."

He pressed the button, zoomed in on Omar's name patch. "The uniform is Harper's, too. Not bad, put on a helmet and face shield, step into the plane and they think he's Harper."

"We need to stop him."

Aaron's gaze swung to the airplane. "Don't suppose we could just shoot the tires and call it a day."

"Shooting the tires won't stop Trygg from releasing the poison. Or killing Sandra." Booker observed the situation through the scope of his rifle. "We need to get on board, change course and destroy the cylinders."

Omar pulled a package from his backpack.

Aaron swore. "He's got C4 explosives. He's going to blow up that plane."

"Damn fool," Booker snapped. "He must not realize Sandra is on board."

"What are you going to do? We can't reach him in time."

"Shoot him." Booker adjusted the scope, bringing Omar's image closer.

"He might be your future father-in-law—"

"Better injured than dead." Booker squeezed the trigger.

Omar cried out; his right leg went out from under him.

"If we survive this, you'd better tell him exactly why you shot him," Aaron warned, running after Booker, gun raised. "Quamar told me what he did to Harper."

Both men sprinted to the aircraft. Aaron knelt beside the doctor.

Omar swore, his hands gripping the bullet wound. "What the hell are you doing here?"

"Saving you." Booker lifted the backpack, checked the contents. "There's no timer. You were going in as a suicide bomber?"

"Trygg has loaded the plane with the best military technology available. Including an EMP shield. An electromagnetic pulse shield will kill any jet or missile instruments within five miles of the airbus."

"I know. I delivered it to him," Aaron muttered.

"You what?" Omar and Booker asked in unison.

"Under orders, damn it," Aaron snapped. "We couldn't sabotage it without blowing the mission. It's fully functional."

Booker swore. "Did you leave us any advantage in your undercover work, Sabra?"

"I got you the girl, didn't I?"

"What girl?" Omar's eyes narrowed. "If you mean Sandra—"

"Later," Booker said, his voice terse. "We have more pressing matters right now."

"All right." Omar nodded stiffly. "Jarek's missiles will never get close enough to bring Trygg down before he reaches Taer," he insisted. "The only way to destroy the cylinders is from the inside. The heat of the explosion will burn off the serum, disrupt the nanites' sensors."

Quickly, Aaron probed the injury, ignored Omar's grunt of pain. "You missed the artery, but caught the bone."

Omar's gaze snapped to Booker. "*You* shot me?"

"You turned at the last moment," Booker clarified, "Otherwise I would have missed the bone, too."

"He shot you to keep you from making a stupid mistake," Aaron added. "Your daughter's on board that plane."

"Sandra?" Omar grabbed Booker's shirt, brought him in close. "I should kill you now. You were supposed to keep her safe."

"I'll save your daughter. Then I'm going to kill her," Booker answered, then pulled away.

"Kill her?" Omar tried to stand. "Get the hell out of here, both of you."

"He wouldn't really kill her. He's just mad that Sandra pushed him out of a helicopter," Aaron answered, then put his hand on Omar's chest to keep him in place. The older man's face paled to a pasty gray. "Stay down. I haven't got the bleeding under control."

"Have you both lost your mind?"

"He has," Aaron commented, then put pressure on the wound with both hands. "He's in love with her."

"Shut up, Sabra." Booker studied the perimeter. "Where are all the guards, Omar?"

"Gone. There were only the three," the older man bit out. "Did Sandra's tracking chip lead you here?"

"Trygg placed the chip on Jim Rayo's dead body," Aaron finished, his hands bloody. He ripped off his belt and placed it as a tourniquet on the leg.

"So you don't know she's there for sure."

"She's there. I know Trygg. He'll want Sandra to watch the deaths. Then he'll kill her." Booker slung the backpack over his shoulder. "I promise you, once I find Sandra, I'll place the explosives for you."

"We need to get him out of here, Booker." Aaron's tone was low, grim. "Now."

"Let's go." Booker hooked his shoulder under Omar's arm, and waited until Aaron did the same. They sprinted, with Omar between them, to the tents nearby.

When they stopped, Omar grabbed Booker's arm, held fast. "I don't want to lose another child."

"You won't. That's why I have to get on that plane."

Aaron checked the leg. Blood saturated the pant leg. "He's losing too much blood."

He glanced at Booker. "If we leave him here, he's a dead man. He's not going to make it out of here on his own."

"Then get him out of here." Booker slipped out from under Omar's arm. "Make your way to the west side of the camp and into the dunes. Find Jarek. Tell them what happened. It will take Trygg's plane a little over an hour after takeoff to reach his target zone over Taer. I'll have the doc out in one hour."

"That's cutting it close, McKnight."

"Check your watch. Not one minute before. If Trygg suspects anything, she'll be the first one to die."

Aaron glanced at the dial, then turned and hoisted Omar up over his shoulder. "Sixty minutes. Check."

The aircraft's engines roared to life.

"Like I said, it's going to be close," Aaron commented. "They're taking off."

"Tell Jarek and Cain I need that hour." Booker dropped the rifle to the ground, shoved his pistol into the backpack. "Then use surface-to-air missiles. If I don't blow the plane with the explosives, I'll disable the EMP shield."

"Here. It's a one-button remote trigger." Omar reached into his pocket and pulled out a small electronic remote. "For the C4. You flip the safety, press the button."

Booker shoved it into his pocket. "Seems simple enough."

BOOKER MANEUVERED UNDER the belly, and found the supply hatch. He raised his gun, fired point-blank at the lock and jerked the door open.

He jumped, grabbed the edge and felt it cut into his fingers. Quickly, he hoisted himself up.

Hydraulic cables moved, gears clicked as the plane picked up speed. Booker scrambled in, dodging crates, following the lighted path of the elongated compartment of wires and storage units.

Pistol in hand, Booker maneuvered to the small steel ladder at the end of the compartment. He swung up, then held on when the airplane slanted steep in its takeoff.

At the top lay another hatch. Slowly, Booker pushed it open, saw a walkway. He climbed through, checked the perimeter for guards, then stopped. Just beyond lay thousands of square feet filled with Plexiglas, sterile areas and computers.

"A moving lab," he murmured. "Why not?"

SANDRA TUGGED AT the handcuffs, her gaze focused on the computer nearby.

"Looking for something?" Lewis Pitman laughed. "No one is here to help you, Sandra. We've cleared out the plane. I've set the computers to automatic. Even my lab technicians have been dispensed of by Trygg's men. It's me, the pilot and Trygg."

"He killed all of the lab people?"

"Cut them down with guns just beyond one of the dunes." Pitman shrugged. "We couldn't risk one of them developing a conscience when we drop the canister over Taer. Better this way."

"And what are you, Lewis?" Sandra scoffed. "What makes you think he won't get rid of you, too?"

"What makes you think I'll give him the opportunity?" Lewis scoffed. "The computer has my key code. Nothing works without my authority. That's my security measure. He needs me."

Then she saw it, the look, the snide, arrogant twist of his mouth. "But you don't need him. Not anymore."

"Not anymore," Lewis agreed, smiling.

"HEADING IS LOCKED in, General. The autopilot is engaged," the pilot stated, satisfied.

Trygg shifted in the copilot's seat and glanced at the young man. His newest recruit. A young kid with close-cropped blond hair and acne still on his cheeks. No more than twenty-five. Barely passed puberty and barely shaving.

"Good job, son." Suddenly, Trygg felt old. And angry. Jim had left him no choice. But killing a friend never sat well with Riorden.

"Thank you, sir," the young soldier replied, then eased back into his chair. "We'll be over our target in fifty-seven minutes."

Trygg took his pistol from beside his seat and stood. "I am sorry you're going to miss it, son." He leveled the pistol and pulled the trigger.

BOOKER HEARD THE BULLET pop just one deck above.

He took the circular stairs two at a time, his pistol up, his heart racing. With quiet steps, Booker made his way into the galley—a gourmet kitchen of steel and black carpet.

A door stood close to the edge of the galley. A storage unit. Booker turned the knob.

A first-aid kit, a portable oxygen tank with mask, several extinguishers. Two parachutes hung from the hooks.

He searched the shelves above, found blankets and pillows. Goggles.

No weapons.

Booker made his way across the tile to the other end of the galley. Slowly, he peered around the corner.

The cockpit door stood ten feet from him on the right. Booker paused. The choice was simple: land the plane or rescue Sandra.

Booker swore, then stepped down the short corridor to the cockpit. He pulled the latch, eased the door open.

The pilot lay slumped back in the seat, dead. Blood saturated his shirt.

"Welcome aboard, Captain." Trygg stepped from the corner, his pistol raised.

THE PLANE JERKED, then slanted. Booker opened his eyes, blinked the blood away.

"Booker," Sandra whispered. "Are you all right?"

Relief filled him. There'd been a small sliver of doubt that he wouldn't reach her in time. He tugged on his hands, found them cuffed above his head. "How long have I been out?"

"No more than five minutes," Trygg answered. "I didn't want you to miss anything."

"We're about twenty minutes out, General." Pitman sat at a nearby computer. "All systems online and focused. I'm loading the weapon."

A missile lowered from the top of the lab, into the floor.

"A bomber bay." Booker swore under his breath. "They built a bomber bay."

"It's more than that. It's aerodynamic dissemination," Sandra whispered. "He developed a smart bomb that has the capability of controlling the release of the nanites into the air. Think of it as a crop-dusting bomb. One that follows a preprogrammed flight pattern."

"Very good, Doctor Haddad," Trygg commented, coming down the stairs.

"So why not shoot us?" Booker prodded. He glanced around, noting Omar's backpack shoved against the nearest console.

"Oh, I will, if I have to, but I'd much rather let you experience the full effect of what I'm trying to accomplish."

"Let me go, General, and we'll experience it together. Side by side." Booker pulled on the handcuffs, rattled them violently and slipped his finger over his watch, finding the shim.

"So you can kill me?" The general laughed. "You are the hero, aren't you? That's why I didn't recruit you years ago."

"Anyone who works for you ends up dead," Booker answered snidely. "Jim Rayo, for instance."

"Other recruits are still alive. Omar Haddad for instance," Trygg added slyly.

"My father?"

"Who do you think signed the obituaries? Helped me with the whole concept of making soldiers invincible?" Trygg questioned. "Ask Booker, Sandra. He'll confirm what I'm saying."

"Why didn't you tell me?" She looked at Booker, the hurt, the rage, painful and obvious.

"Probably the same reason why he didn't tell you your serum killed his wife and child."

"You murdered them, not Sandra," Booker replied, his voice hard.

"Emily?" Sandra paled. Her gaze sought Booker's.

Booker refused to look at her. "The doc had nothing to do with it—"

"Look at her face, McKnight," Trygg snapped. "She even knows you're lying. She developed CIRCADIAN. The same weapon that's about to kill her family. Ironic really."

"Ironic?" Sandra whispered.

"I read your profile." Trygg smiled, vicious. "You want your father's approval. You want to be just like him. Now look at you, helping in the demise of your family. The ones he wasn't able to destroy himself."

Nausea swelled; bile caught at the back of her throat.

"Like father, like daughter," Trygg added. "He'll be so proud."

"Don't listen to him, Doc," Booker ordered.

"And who should I listen to? You?" Sandra demanded. "Emily hemorrhaged to death but it wasn't because of the miscarriage. She was on the base."

"Doc—"

"Tell me I'm wrong!"

"She was there. But it's not your fault," Booker insisted.

"I think I should get some of the credit." Lewis

Pitman spoke from a few feet away. "I'm the one who changed the programming on the carbon nanites."

"What are you talking about?" she argued. "The reports showed no change…"

"He falsified his reports," Trygg explained.

Sandra's eyes snapped to Trygg's. "Lewis couldn't have done that on his own. He needed—"

"I authorized everything," Trygg admitted.

"Senator Harper supported him. They made quite a team," Booker added.

"The DNA programming in the sensors malfunctioned in one of the first series of experiments," Lewis inserted. "The nanites ignored the unhealthy cells and attacked the healthy ones, causing the breakdown of tissues. I took the results to Trygg."

"Enemies slain by one type of nanite, while our soldiers are saved by the other," Trygg commented with satisfaction.

"The best of both worlds," Sandra reasoned aloud. But with the realization came anger. "If you are relying on Pitman to reconstruct my equations, he hasn't the ability."

"Then I will find someone who does," Trygg countered.

"I can reconstruct them." Lewis stood, his face mottled with anger. "And improve on your equations. Accelerate the process, strengthen the results."

He reached over the console, punched the security

code. A vault slid open. He pointed to the cylinders. "See those? They will be obsolete when I finish."

"Be careful, Lewis," Booker advised. "Rayo, Harper and the pilot are all dead. You can easily outlive your usefulness, too."

"The pilot's dead?" Pitman's head shot up, his eyes on Trygg.

"This information is a little premature." Trygg sighed. "But true. The airplane is on autopilot."

"Have you lost your mind? Who is going to land us?"

"Me," Trygg stated. "So I guess you'd better make sure I stay alive."

Lewis glanced at the vault, realized his mistake.

"But now that you've opened the vault, I guess I don't need you anymore, do I, Lewis?"

Lewis dived for the cylinders. A shot rang out. Lewis stiffened. A crimson target spread over the back of his white lab coat.

Slowly, he slid to the ground.

"You're going to do this on your own?" Sandra asked.

Trygg stepped toward Sandra and grabbed her chin. "There are far more scientists out there like Pitman, who can be bought, than there are of you—who can't."

Booker broke free of the cuffs, grabbed the chains and kicked Trygg, knocking the gun free from his hand. Trygg bounced off the equipment, forced himself back on his feet.

"We both know how this is going to end." Trygg stumbled back, grabbed one of the cylinders. He twisted the top, held it in place. "If you move an inch, I'm going to release this canister into the air." He reached down and grabbed Omar's backpack, then with one hand, shoved two cylinders into its pocket.

"Now, I'm going to walk past the good doctor and you," he warned, and slung the strap over his shoulder. "Then up those stairs. And you're going to let me do it. Because if you don't, I'll release the nanites."

Chapter Eighteen

"Why did you let him go?"

"Because by the time he gets anywhere, this plane will be blown up," Booker said, and quickly unlocked her cuffs. "Did you get a good look at the computer controls?"

"Yes," She shook out her arms, rubbed her wrists, then hurried over to the console. "The lab is rigged for biological contamination. If he releases the serum, a biohazard alarm will engage."

"Where's the EMP shield?"

"By the radar." She looked at the screen, saw the blips. "Three missiles are eight minutes out, Booker. They will enter the EMP zone..." She grabbed his wrist, glanced at his watch. "In two minutes."

"Can you shut down the EMP shield?"

"Not without a ten-digit code." She looked at the screen. "It will shut down automatically when the bomb is released to keep the tracking system from malfunctioning."

Booker picked up Trygg's pistol, and leveled it at the console. "Step back."

When she did, he fired several shots.

Sparks flew; lights blinked off.

"That did it." Sandra checked the radar. "The missiles are seven minutes out."

"Right." He shoved the pistol in his back waistband. "Let's go."

"Wait a minute." Sandra grabbed the last cylinder, held it tight in her hand.

"Is that necessary?"

"Yes." Sandra's face was set, determined.

Booker grabbed her by the shoulders and pulled her close. "I know you heard a lot of information from Trygg, Doc. But don't believe it all. Your father was on his way into this plane to destroy it with explosives. When he found out you were on board, he trusted me to save you and take care of Trygg."

"Thanks." She kissed him softly on the mouth. "So where are we going?"

"Cargo. Front of the plane. There are parachutes."

"The same place where Trygg is heading?"

"Probably."

"Is that necessary?" she asked, using his own words from a moment ago.

"Yes."

THEY FOUND HIM AT the galley's emergency exit. He'd looped the backpack over his chest, strapped the parachute on his back, the canister in his hand.

"Time to say goodbye, Doctor Haddad." He jerked the latch, watched the door blow out into the air.

"Here's your serum." Trygg threw the canister, then jumped out of the plane.

The canister burst open at Booker's feet. Within seconds, alarms sounded. Booker snagged the oxygen tank from the galley cupboard, pushed it onto Sandra's face. "No!"

Her hands slapped at his arms. He grabbed her wrists, held them still.

"Listen to me! We don't have time." He took a breath, knowing he was breathing in a death sentence.

Sandra grabbed his shirt, hung on. "Booker! Don't!"

"I can't watch you die, Sandra."

"So you're going to make me watch you." Tears filled her eyes, ran down her face.

"Trygg left one parachute." Booker grabbed it from the galley closet, slipped it over her back and buckled it.

"Hold on to me. We'll go tandem," she pleaded. "If we get you to the hospital, I might be able to reverse the damage."

"All right. Tandem," he agreed. He wrapped her in his arms, hugged her close.

"I love you, Booker." She cupped his cheek, waited.

He caught her hand and pressed it to his skin but said nothing.

"One, two, three. Go!" Booker stepped out of her arms and shoved Sandra out the open hatch.

"I love you, too, Doc," he murmured. Without another thought, he jumped into the open air, gun in hand.

Booker dived, his arms tucked at his side. Air rushed at him. He searched for Trygg.

A parachute opened below. Trygg's…

He hit the man in the back, rolled with him in the air. Trygg grabbed Booker's throat. But Booker already had his hand in the backpack.

The steel of the cylinders hit his hand. He grabbed them, then shoved Trygg away with his knees.

Trygg scrambled for balance, but he was too late.

Booker reached into his pocket, flipped the safety and hit the remote button.

Trygg exploded into a fireball.

Booker spread his arms, catching wind, and shot up. Suddenly, Sandra appeared, grabbed him midair.

He looped his arms into her straps and nodded.

She pulled the toggle and the chute popped open.

"Don't you dare die on me, McKnight!"

Booker took the impact of the touchdown. Both grappled for a moment against the wind shear and the parachute. He pulled the cord, releasing the chute across the desert.

"Hold on, Booker. They'll find us and I'll figure out how to save you."

"Doesn't matter now, Doc," Booker answered, suddenly tired. "You're safe. Trygg's dead."

It took three hours for the helicopter to find them. An hour of which Booker lay unconscious in Sandra's arms.

She'd never felt so helpless in her life.

Finally, the spotlight hit her. She waved her arms. "Hurry," she whispered, knowing they couldn't hear her over the helicopter's blades.

As soon as it settled, Quamar and Aaron jumped from its cockpit.

"I need a stretcher!" Sandra screamed. Aaron turned back, waved at two men in the helicopter.

"What happened?"

"He breathed in the nanites."

"Then there's nothing we can do, Sandra," Quamar said quietly.

"I can save him, Quamar," Sandra insisted. "It wasn't the serum that killed Booker's wife. It was the nanites. Pitman skewed the programming to cause damage. I just need to find someone who is experienced in reprogramming the nanites."

"Kate MacAlister is in Taer. She flew in to take charge of disaster protocol, just in case the CIRCDIAN was released." Quamar took his phone out of his pocket. "I'll have her meet us at the hospital."

It took another hour to reach the hospital. "His pulse is weak," Aaron stated, coming up on the women. He and Quamar handed Booker over to the waiting interns. "His breathing is erratic. I gave him oxygen."

"He's fighting the onslaught. The body is moving into a self-induced coma," Sandra explained, her tone urgent.

Kate MacAlister met them at the main entrance. "We have the surgery room ready. Number two."

"Thank you." Sandra waved two nurses to her side. "I need two interns. And the patient prepped. I want him ready when we're done. No medication. Nothing. Not even for the pain. They'll interfere with my nanites."

Two interns carried Booker down the hallway on the stretcher. She turned to Kate. "It's over four hours."

"How many hours do we have?"

"Twelve more. Outside. Before the damage is irreparable." Sandra turned to the older woman. "I know I don't deserve your help, but Booker needs it…" Her voice cracked. "I'm so sorry, Kate."

"Forgiven. Years ago." Kate gave her a swift hug. "Now what do you need me to do?"

"The nanites. They were the defective part of

the procedure," Sandra explained. "The flaw was in Pitman's design. If we make the corrections, I can counteract the bad nanites with good nanites that match Booker's DNA."

"A war of nanites in his body?" Kate asked. "Will he survive that?"

"I don't know," she said truthfully. "But he won't survive otherwise."

"Is Trygg's lab still intact?" Kate asked.

"No."

"We need access to a nanite lab," Kate said, thinking. "Nearest is London."

"Just so happens I know the Prime Minister," Quamar said grimly. "Jordan Beck."

"That will work," Kate said urgently. "Still, it will be close."

"I'll get started on the DNA matching," Sandra insisted. "Once his organs start shutting down, they might not be strong enough to counter and survive the battle."

"He'll need blood. And a lot of it," Kate insisted.

"His blood type is rare," Sandra remembered. "Call ahead, Quamar, tell them we need AB negative."

"And if they don't have enough on hand?" Quamar warned.

Aaron stepped up, his features set. "He can have all he wants of mine."

"AB negative?" Sandra demanded.

"Yes, ma'am," Aaron replied. "And this one is on the house."

Chapter Nineteen

Two months later

The Al Asheera's camp wound along the lowest ridge, a snake of canvas tents interspersed with wagons, small herds of goats and camels.

The smell of coffee and baking bread drifted on the wind and reached Booker on the cliff above.

His stomach tightened.

He'd been traveling by horse for two days with little food and less sleep.

He peered through his binoculars.

It had been two months since they took Trygg down. Two months since Sandra forced the internal nanite war inside him. And saved his life.

For the first week or so, he'd felt like a human punching bag. Kate MacAlister had told him just how close he'd come to dying. How hard Sandra fought to save him.

Now it was his turn to fight for her.

"Let's go, Sam," Booker murmured and nudged his horse down the slope.

Less than an hour past dawn, but the camp was active. The men were lighting fires, tending to the stock. The woman tended to the children, and prepared the morning meal.

He slid out of the saddle and onto the ground, then tethered his horse on a loose caravan wheel.

"Are you here for something, McKnight?" Aaron Sabra strolled over from a nearby tent. "Or someone?"

"Very funny, Sabra. Where is she?" Booker glanced at the rifle holstered in the saddle, left it there and swung around. "Where is the doc?"

"Who told you she was here?" Aaron sipped some of his coffee.

"Kate," Booker replied, not amused. "I hope you've kept her safe."

"I've kept her busy." Aaron smiled into his cup. "The only one she needs to be kept safe from is you."

"Busy doing what?"

"She's a doctor. What do you think?"

Booker stepped forward. "So help me, God, if she gets sick, I'll—"

"You'll what? Hurt me?" Aaron's eyes went slate-gray. "Do you really think anything my people could do would hurt her any more than you have already?"

"I'm not here to hurt her. I'm here to make things

right." But the fact she'd been suffering didn't sit well with Booker.

"Fair enough." Aaron lifted a negligent shoulder. "But she's kept herself busy with my people."

"Your people?"

"Yes," Aaron explained. "Jon Mercer has persuaded me to help rebuild the Al Asheera into a productive tribe. One that works with Jarek, instead of against him."

"And Sandra?"

"She's spent her days vaccinating the young, healing the sick, comforting the elderly. She's even delivered a few babies over the last couple of weeks."

"I want to see her."

"She went for a walk," Aaron replied. "You'll find her by the rocks, just outside of camp."

"Alone?"

"Usually," Aaron said, coughing to keep from laughing. "Just be back before noon meal. My people have grown fond of her, and will expect her for the noon meal."

"I do not think this will take four hours—"

"You don't think this is going to be easy, do you, McKnight?" Aaron laughed this time. The deep, hearty laugh of someone who'd been in the same quandary. "Groveling to the woman you love is a long, drawn-out process."

"For the record, Sabra?" Booker swung back up

on Sam. "Your job protecting Sandra is over. For the rest of your life. Understood?"

"Understood," Aaron answered, grinning. "For your sake, I hope she's alone."

"Why?"

"If you have to grovel, you're not going to want an audience."

SANDRA SAT CROSS-LEGGED on the highest boulder, her gaze steady on the Sahara. The sun danced over the horizon, spinning gold from sand, turquoise from the cool morning air and blue skies.

A new day.

She rested her hands across her stomach, breathed deep to settle the flutter of nervousness, the touch of nausea.

A new beginning.

The wind tugged at her hair, whipped her tiered skirt around her legs. She brought her knees up to her chest, held her skirt close with her arms.

She'd spent the past two months amongst the Al Asheera. Two months getting to know their way of life, and their families and bringing their babies into the world, and sometimes—she smiled—their livestock.

Her free time she'd spent on the boulders, sometimes talking with Aaron or one of the camp women, but mostly alone—listening to the wind, the quiet hum of her thoughts.

Yet nothing eased her doubts, the nagging ache in her heart.

Nothing blocked the image of Booker, pale and half-dead, from her mind.

It had been close. His kidneys had shut down, his spleen hemorrhaged. The first she saved, the second she couldn't.

But he'd pulled through and healed quickly.

She leaned back on her hands, closed her eyes, lost herself in the heat of the sun.

The whistle, a low rendition of "You Are My Sunshine," drifted over the boulder.

Her eyes blinked open. "Go away, Booker."

Instead, he moved closer. "Now, Doc," Booker drawled with his best Texan accent. "You know if I were that easy, we wouldn't be in this predicament. You would have stuck it out at the hospital until I woke up."

"We've said everything that needed saying in the plane," Sandra shot back, her gaze locking on his.

His features had darkened, the lines on his face deepened, with fatigue or worry, she couldn't be sure. He'd lost weight, grown whiskers, but neither dulled the sharp blue irises that drifted over her.

"You said all you needed to say," Booker corrected softly. "And all I needed to hear."

"And you said nothing."

"I was a little busy at the time, sweetheart," Booker reasoned, his mouth twisting with amusement.

"You lost your chance," she managed, her voice calm. But her fingers trembled, her heart stumbled. "Shouldn't you be at the palace?"

"I'm exactly where I want to be."

"Aaron told me that Jarek wants you back as his security consultant."

"I turned him down," Booker replied. "I'm heading back to the States."

"Oh." Something sharp hit Sandra in the chest. So she was a loose end. And he was leaving. So be it.

She drew her knees back up, tightened her arms around her legs. "I guess we both got what we wanted." She rocked, just a bit. To make the hurt go away.

"Not even close." Booker settled next her. "Have you talked with your parents?"

Sandra stared off into the distance. "No. They're on a long-needed vacation. The inquest was fast and efficient. President Mercer made sure of it."

"He was found innocent on all counts of treason," Booker remembered. "I heard it on the news."

"Once my father's involvement became public, he seemed relieved. My mother has been supportive. My brother, too."

"And you?"

Sandra shrugged. "I realize he had no choice. But when he recruited me to work for Trygg—"

"He didn't give you a choice," Booker finished, understanding. "You would have made the same decision, Doc. You would have helped Jonathon Mercer."

"I would have," Sandra admitted. "But if my father had told me what Trygg was from the beginning…"

She gave in to the urge and settled her chin on her knees. "So many died, Booker. I can't help thinking that if my father had only trusted me, your men, Emily and your baby…"

"Time to move on, Doc," he said, studying the horizon. "Time to live our life for ourselves."

"I don't know if I can, Booker. Not yet."

"I flew out to meet with them, you know. Your parents."

"You flew all the way out to Amsterdam?"

"Your father and I had some things to settle. About Trygg. My men. You."

"My father never discusses his family."

"He loves you, Doc. He didn't tell you about Trygg because he was trying to protect you. Kate was supposed to be the point person on Trygg but it never materialized. If they hadn't pulled her from the project, Trygg would've killed Kate just like he killed Jim Rayo's wife and all the others."

Sandra frowned, but said nothing.

"By the time Kate left, it was obvious to your father you worshipped the ground Trygg walked on. And at that time you and your father were barely on speaking terms. If he had told you that Trygg was a traitor, would you have believed him?"

Her head shot up. "Yes," she defended.

Booker's eyebrow rose.

Sandra sighed, then let her chin drop to her knees again. "Probably not."

"You need to talk with him, Doc. You need to forgive him. Life is too short to carry that kind of anguish inside."

Tears pricked at her eyes; her breath lumped in her chest. She would, too. She loved her father too much to do anything else. Still, she would need time to trust, but hopefully, that too would come.

"Doc, you didn't spend your whole life living up to Andon's memory. You spent your whole life living through your father's guilt," Booker pointed out softly. He draped his arm over her shoulders, pulled her close. "Guilt that he is finally coming to terms with. Don't you think it's time you come to terms with your own and not take the twenty-five years it took your father?"

The lump thickened until it rose to the back of her throat. "And you? Your guilt is gone?"

He took her chin, tilted it until they were nose to nose. "I'm working on it."

"How?" Her breath caught, and love jolted through his chest, squeezed his heart.

Instinctively, he drew her closer until they were

chest to chest, heartbeat to heartbeat. "I contacted my grandfather."

"You did?" One hand went to his chest, stopping him from drawing her in, from making her believe.

The other went to her stomach, to protect, or maybe to wish...

"Why did you see your grandfather?"

"I don't know," Booker admitted. His hand slid up her spine, absently massaging the tension from her shoulders. "After I talked with your father, I found myself on my grandfather's doorstep."

"Was he happy to see you?"

"*Shocked* would be a better word," Booker replied. His grandfather had not changed much over the years. Thin and frail, with very little hair, but the same sharp blue eyes.

"What happened?"

"He wants me to run his company. He's been saving it for me in case I came around."

"Are you?" she demanded, her eyes wide, unbelieving again. "Coming around, I mean."

"Who knows?" He paused, then pulled back until their eyes met. A grin spread slowly across his mouth.

Her heart bumped.

"Yes, actually. I am."

"You lost me, Booker." Sandra shook her head, confused. "You're going to run his company?"

"My grandfather offered to make his overseas

headquarters here in Taer. Fifteen hundred people will be given jobs, and more than twice that number will relocate from the States," Booker acknowledged. "It will mean a lot of traveling, since the main headquarters will remain in Texas. Six months here. Six months there."

"That's quite a bargaining chip."

"Both will have a research department."

Sandra quirked an eyebrow. The sadness drowned in a thick haze of sudden anger. "I have a job. I don't need you to find me one, Booker."

"You're going to continue to work for Jarek as his royal physician?"

"Most likely. He needs someone to replace my father, at least temporarily." But she wasn't sure. There was more than just herself to consider now. "I certainly don't want to work for you. Or be anywhere near you for that matter. I don't think we can go back, Booker. Too much has happened. There's still too many secrets. And even more regrets."

Fear clamped in his gut, twisting his insides. "I think I fell in love with you the moment I saw you in the desert," he admitted quietly.

Sandra stiffened, not sure she'd heard his words correctly.

"We were at the oil drill site in Taer. You were standing there, across the sand. In a hat, sunglasses—" he glanced at her shirt and pants "—the same khakis."

"They're comfortable," Sandra quipped, then frowned. "I remember that day, though. One of your men had been injured. He caught his leg in one of the winch chains."

"I hadn't been that nervous since—" He swore silently. "Hell, I've never been that nervous. Except for now."

"Booker, this..." She waved her hand between them. "It will go away. It has to."

"It hasn't for four years, Doc."

"Why now?" Sandra demanded. "Why couldn't you have said all of this a year ago? Or even two months ago in the cave when we made love."

When we conceived our baby, she added silently.

"When I married Emily, I thought I loved her. I thought she was all I wanted. Stability, comfort, family."

"It was there. You just didn't have enough time with her," Sandra insisted. "We stole that away from you."

"No," Booker denied. "You can't steal something that never existed in the first place."

"What do you mean?"

Booker took Sandra's hand. The calluses, the heated grip, invaded the dark part of her heart. She couldn't bring up the strength to tug free.

"Emily was the only child of an overindulgent father. She was too selfish, too vain to care about anything other than herself," Booker told her. "Sandra, Em wasn't coming to tell me she was overjoyed at being pregnant. She was coming to tell me she didn't want my baby. She never wanted to get pregnant. The pregnancy wasn't planned."

He paused for a moment. "She was leaving me. Her bags were packed and in the trunk of her car. She hated me enough to tell me in person that she was filing for a divorce and getting rid of my baby."

His voice rasped out the last word. Tears pricked at Sandra's eyes. She blinked them away.

"It took me all these years to sort it out in my mind," Booker explained. "I think somehow, when I first met Emily, I compared her to my mother. An heiress of sorts, who would defy her father for an undying love."

"But Emily wasn't like your mom."

"No, she married me on a whim. To get back at her father, I'm sure," Booker admitted. "Their relationship was extreme in all emotions. Anger, love."

"She still didn't deserve to die, Booker."

"No, she didn't." He brought Sandra's hand to his cheek, pressed a soft kiss on her wrist.

Her pulse quickened, her fingers caressed the whiskers, the slant of his jaw. It was then she understood she'd never be able to stop loving this man.

But she could still walk away.

"The revenge I took on Trygg wasn't out of love for Emily or for my men, Sandra," Booker admitted. "It was born from anger, guilt...pride. Loyalty maybe. But never love."

When she looked away, he took her chin between his thumb and forefinger and turned her face back to his. "But when he took you? The rage, the fear I felt, rocked me to the core. I would have avenged you. And it would have been out of love."

"I don't want you to avenge me." This time Sandra did tug free. She rose to her feet, dusted off the back of her skirt. "It wouldn't work, Booker. Every time we looked at each other, we'd remember what brought us together."

"Damn right it will," Booker replied, grabbing her hand to keep her from leaving. "And I don't ever want to forget."

Surprised, she looked at him. "What?"

"I hope I never forget." He tugged her hand, catching her in his arms and across his lap. Before she could move away, he hugged her to his chest. "You almost died on me, Doc. So many times, I've lost count."

"Five," she admitted, somewhat reluctantly. "Six, if you include the moment on the plane when you couldn't say you loved me."

"I was fighting my fear of losing you," Booker admitted. He linked his fingers with hers, left them resting across her belly. "If I'd said the words out loud, I wouldn't have been able to let you go."

"You didn't *let* me go—you threw me out of the

plane," Sandra murmured. "Can't get more decisive than that."

"You kicked me out of a helicopter first," he reminded her with a smile. "I love you, Doc. And if it takes me our lifetime together to convince you, so be it."

"It just might." Her voice hitched; her heart fluttered. "Just because I want you around for a lifetime, Booker."

He let out a long sigh. The vibration rumbled against her ear, making her want to sink farther into his chest.

"Fine with me." He tipped her chin up, kissed her softly on the lips. "I want to raise a family with you and grow old together."

"The family part is taken care of," she whispered, the words bursting from her heart, shining through the sheen of tears in her eyes. "I would say in about seven months."

Booker slid his hand over her stomach with gentle fingers. "And the growing old together?"

She laughed and hugged him close. "I guess that will happen if we stay away from high places."

* * * * *

LARGER-PRINT BOOKS!
GET 2 FREE LARGER-PRINT NOVELS PLUS
2 FREE GIFTS!

HARLEQUIN®

INTRIGUE®

BREATHTAKING ROMANTIC SUSPENSE

YES! Please send me 2 FREE LARGER-PRINT Harlequin Intrigue® novels and my 2 FREE gifts (gifts are worth about $10). After receiving them, if I don't wish to receive any more books, I can return the shipping statement marked "cancel." If I don't cancel, I will receive 6 brand-new novels every month and be billed just $5.49 per book in the U.S. or $5.99 per book in Canada. That's a saving of at least 13% off the cover price! It's quite a bargain! Shipping and handling is just 50¢ per book in the U.S. and 75¢ per book in Canada.* I understand that accepting the 2 free books and gifts places me under no obligation to buy anything. I can always return a shipment and cancel at any time. Even if I never buy another book, the two free books and gifts are mine to keep forever.

199/399 HDN F42Y

Name _____ (PLEASE PRINT)

Address _____ Apt. #

City _____ State/Prov. _____ Zip/Postal Code

Signature (if under 18, a parent or guardian must sign)

Mail to the Harlequin® Reader Service:
IN U.S.A.: P.O. Box 1867, Buffalo, NY 14240-1867
IN CANADA: P.O. Box 609, Fort Erie, Ontario L2A 5X3

**Are you a subscriber to Harlequin Intrigue books
and want to receive the larger-print edition?
Call 1-800-873-8635 today or visit www.ReaderService.com.**

* Terms and prices subject to change without notice. Prices do not include applicable taxes. Sales tax applicable in N.Y. Canadian residents will be charged applicable taxes. Offer not valid in Quebec. This offer is limited to one order per household. Not valid for current subscribers to Harlequin Intrigue Larger-Print books. All orders subject to credit approval. Credit or debit balances in a customer's account(s) may be offset by any other outstanding balance owed by or to the customer. Please allow 4 to 6 weeks for delivery. Offer available while quantities last.

Your Privacy—The Harlequin® Reader Service is committed to protecting your privacy. Our Privacy Policy is available online at www.ReaderService.com or upon request from the Harlequin Reader Service.

We make a portion of our mailing list available to reputable third parties that offer products we believe may interest you. If you prefer that we not exchange your name with third parties, or if you wish to clarify or modify your communication preferences, please visit us at www.ReaderService.com/consumerschoice or write to us at Harlequin Reader Service Preference Service, P.O. Box 9062, Buffalo, NY 14269. Include your complete name and address.

HILP13R

Reader Service.com

Manage your account online!

- Review your order history
- Manage your payments
- Update your address

*We've designed
the Harlequin® Reader Service
website just for you.*

Enjoy all the features!

- Reader excerpts from any series
- Respond to mailings and special monthly offers
- Discover new series available to you
- Browse the Bonus Bucks catalog
- Share your feedback

Visit us at:
ReaderService.com

RS13